Praise for *The Valley of Vengeful Ghosts*

"This book has all the weirdness, madness, and surreal beauty we've come to expect of Kim Fu's work. Part psychological horror, part existential philosophy, and a whole lot of ghosts—a chilling and pitch perfect experience, I read it in one feverish dream."

—SUSIE YANG,
AUTHOR OF *WHITE IVY*

"I was utterly enthralled by Kim Fu's *The Valley of Vengeful Ghosts*, a brilliantly written tale of grief, loneliness, and the horrors of real estate. Images from this novel will probably haunt me forever. A bold and searing work by a writer working at the top of their game."

—KATE FOLK,
AUTHOR OF *SKY DADDY*

"A story addictive enough to devour in one sitting, *The Valley of Vengeful Ghosts* introduces a world in which quotidian fears bloom luridly into nightmare. Through Eleanor's eyes, twenty-first century terrors are considered in all their varied forms: technological interference, the violence of loneliness, and worst, the kinds of natural and psychological damage we've brought upon ourselves. I looked up from this book and saw everything around me in higher definition."

—LUCY TAN,
AUTHOR OF *WHAT WE WERE PROMISED*

"Gorgeous and profoundly moving, Kim Fu's *The Valley of Vengeful Ghosts* lays bare the lonely abyss of grief and all of its disorienting contours. Just when I thought I would drown, she brought me to the surface, gasping for air. An extraordinary and unforgettable novel."

—TALIA LAKSHMI KOLLURI,
AUTHOR OF *WHAT WE FED TO THE MANTICORE*

PRAISE FOR KIM FU

"Fu's fiction is mesmerizing."

—R.O. KWON,
AUTHOR OF *EXHIBIT*

"Kim Fu writes with grace, wit, mischief, daring, and her own deep weird phosphorescent understanding."

—KEVIN BROCKMEIER,
AUTHOR OF *THE GHOST VARIATIONS*

"Kim Fu's talent is singularly inventive, her every sentence a surprise and an adventure."

—DANYA KUKAFKA,
AUTHOR OF *NOTES ON AN EXECUTION*

THE VALLEY OF VENGEFUL GHOSTS

Also by Kim Fu

Lesser Known Monsters of the 21st Century

The Lost Girls of Camp Forevermore

How Festive the Ambulance

For Today I Am a Boy

THE VALLEY OF VENGEFUL GHOSTS

a novel

Kim Fu

Tin House
A zando IMPRINT
NEW YORK

Tin House

Tin House is an imprint of Zando.
zandoprojects.com

First US Edition 2026
Manufacturing by Lake Book Manufacturing
Cover and text design by Beth Steidle

Library of Congress Cataloging-in-Publication Data is available.

978-1-963108-69-9 (paperback)
978-1-963108-77-4 (ebook)

10 9 8 7 6 5 4 3 2 1

Manufactured in the United States of America

THE VALLEY OF VENGEFUL GHOSTS

From her roof, Eleanor pictures the community that will never be. In her mind, the promised crews arrive with the rewilding of late spring, when the rivers are flush with ordinary snowmelt, their banks holding strong, and the hearts of invasive daisies beam as yellow as the backhoe. A year of frenzied construction follows, the once silent valley filled with movement and noise—hammers, screaming electric saws; barked, anxious orders as the windows are lifted into place by crane—until, at last, the houses are finished.

She imagines each home filled, one by one, with a family. Eleanor, as the first resident, becomes a kind of leader, den mother, witch. She appears on the doorstep of the second people to move in, bearing a pie—she will learn to make pie—and then, only days later, they go together to the house of the next family to arrive. Three households then greet the fourth, descending upon them as they unload furniture from a rented truck, bearing gifts like the three wise men: a casserole, a potted succulent, and Eleanor's now-signature pie. And so on, like children playing sardines, the welcome party grows, until an entire neighborhood stands waiting, throngs lining the streets, as the final family drives down from the mountain road. They are families of every configuration, children of every age, adults single, widowed, retired, coupled, throupled. They surround the last empty house, applauding, the children laughing and running between connected yards, loose dogs at their heels.

They form a village made intimate by isolation. Eleanor's kitchen becomes a makeshift meeting hall, where they debate earnestly over whether to pave the gravel roads, whether to invest together in solar panels for their roofs, whether the man who keeps chickens in his yard should be allowed to have a rooster—the crowing will echo, they note. People bring their own folding chairs, stand in the corners, and Eleanor brews pot after pot of coffee. A few people stay back at the end to wash the mugs, to gossip and debrief. It's these lingerers, mostly women, twisting dishrags inside each mug, sealing unfinished coffee cake in cling wrap, who make the final decisions.

The surrounding forest recovers, encroaches, the borders between their world and the natural one playfully blurring, fuzzy again with native wildflowers and saplings, the summer drone of bees. Eleanor will stand at the juncture between roads and call, "I'm going into town. Anyone need anything?" and people will call back from their porches, yell down from their windows. They will care for one another's babies and elders and ill, share leftovers, wander house to house like cats. A child learning to play the trumpet will amuse and annoy everyone, the spit-choked honking and whistling refining over weeks and months to a clear, piercing note in the night.

If only, that first day Eleanor saw the house, she'd hesitated longer, made a lower offer. If only one of Matt's kids had woken up that morning with the flu, or an accident had blocked off the highway, or the rains had started sooner, washing out the mountain road. If only she'd never come at all.

1

Eleanor struggled to push past the weight of the two doors of her apartment building, the inner wooden door and the latticed iron security door, the wind against her. It was the first of October, and the mild, dry September already felt distant, a brief burst of fiery color crushed underfoot, replaced by a wet, enduring gray, barreling toward winter. How strange, everyone said, that the change had happened so early, so fast. (How strange, they'd said the year before, when it came late, almost not at all, in an endless, killing summer.) Against the gloom—the slush of rotting leaves clogging the storm drains, the soaked brown brick of her building, the algae-covered sidewalk, the low, overcast sky—Matt's car at the curb stood out, silver and sleekly shining.

He stood beside it with his hands clasped in front of him, his back straight, in a cornflower-blue suit—a playful, daytime color—with no tie. His thick hair was slicked back, coiffed high off his forehead. He smiled toothily as she approached. He held his hand out for a shake, and a large watch slid out of his jacket sleeve, the band and bezel the same chrome brightness as his car.

Matt pumped Eleanor's hand with vigor. "A pleasure," he said. The tops of his brown loafers shone, but the heels were caked in mud, the shoes a poor choice for the weather. He took a business card out of a card holder—ridged, yet more silver—and passed it to her. "Matt Halset."

"Eleanor Fan." Eleanor had not made an effort to look like anything other than what she was. She wore an olive-green sweater with holes worn at the waist and cuffs, a sweater that she liked for the color, though the rough wool gave her hives if she wore it against her bare skin. Her hair was in a low, practical bun. She tucked his card into the back pocket of her jeans, already knowing she'd lose it.

Matt opened the passenger-side door for her. She climbed in. The leather interior was immaculate. Her boots dragged mud and errant leaves onto the floor mat.

The road running in front of her building was quiet for midmorning on a Sunday. They sped off without having to merge. Matt asked if the temperature was okay, if she was too hot or cold, and she murmured that she was fine. "So tell me about your work with Mary," he said. "I gather you've seen a lot of places?"

He managed to look both at her and at the road, glancing rapidly back and forth, which she disliked. She turned to the window. "Yes, Mary was very patient with me. I think my expectations were a little unreasonable at the beginning."

Matt laughed. He had a loud laugh. "Oh, every first-time homebuyer is *a little unreasonable* at first. And to be frank, it's not a great time to buy. Inventory is low, interest rates are high. It can be a bit of a shock, seeing what your money buys today."

"How is Mary?" Eleanor was surprised at the wistfulness in her voice. She hadn't particularly liked Mary, but already she liked Matt less.

"Last I heard, the baby hadn't come yet, but it should be any day now. I'm honored she referred you to me." He took the cloverleaf highway entrance at speed, the engine making a stealthy, expensive purr, the force pressing Eleanor's body against the door. "Mary sent along an idea of what you're looking for, but I'm excited to get to know you better. There are some things that don't translate to checkboxes and search terms, you know?" Eleanor made a vague sound of assent. "What made you want to take the leap?"

"I'm sorry?"

"Into buying your first home."

"Oh. My mother—" Eleanor began. Her eyes pinched shut. She imagined her mother were with them, in the back seat. No, Lele would have sat up front, leaning across the console, chatting amicably with Matt. Leading the conversation, sizing him up. Eleanor would be in the back. She opened her eyes and glanced over her shoulder, disappointed not to see herself there. To see her own neck lolling against one of the back headrests, her features peaceful and soft. Daydreaming, nearly asleep.

"My mother died," she said, finally. "It was her idea. She told me to buy a house with my inheritance. Before she passed, she made sure that when everything was settled, there would be enough left for a down payment." At the time, this had seemed like the least important of her mother's instructions, all dictated from bed—usually in the morning, around her second round of medications. The hours she was most alert, the horrors of the night in retreat. But now it was the only thing Eleanor had left to do, the last of Lele's orders.

"I'm sorry to hear about your mother," Matt said, not missing a beat. He drove with one hand, diving between lanes. "I'm sure she would be happy to know she could help you in this way. Oh, I meant to tell you—you're welcome to bring someone along next time. A friend, a family member. It's good to have more eyes on a place, someone to bounce your thoughts off of."

When she didn't respond—there was no such person—he continued, "And you offered on a place before, with Mary? Is that right?"

"Four."

"Four—" Matt swept the car into the left lane. The car behind honked. "You were outbid four times? On four different places?"

"Yes."

After a pause, he said, "That's not that uncommon, these days. But it must have been very frustrating. I'm glad you haven't given up! We'll find you the perfect home yet." A new crease had appeared on Matt's forehead. "Normally I try to line up at least a few listings in one day, but as I said, there's not a lot out there right now, and this place is a bit of a drive. But it's really something special. I think you'll love it."

They made idle conversation about the city: the ever-worsening weather, the underfunded transit system, the overloaded airport. The number and ages of Matt's children, where and how he met his wife. He talked about the local football team for a long, uninterrupted stretch, seemingly aware that he was just filling the silence, undeterred by her lack of enthusiasm.

"Can you remind me what you do for work?" he asked.

"I'm a therapist."

"Ah. I don't think Mary mentioned that. I never would have guessed." Quickly, as though realizing he might have offended her, he added, "Is your office downtown? The commute won't be as bad as it seems, I promise."

"I gave up my office a few years ago. I only do virtual sessions from home now."

They exited the highway directly onto the main street of a one-road former mining town, one of the last in a string of small towns running parallel to the highway, the towns shrinking and getting farther apart as they'd continued east. The town sign straddled a short stretch of disconnected train track, alongside a piece of mining machinery painted over in a dull brass. *Welcome to Bering Rock!*

They reached the other end of town after only a few minutes, a few blocks of brown storefront awnings giving way to small industrial lots. After the final building—a warehouse circled by sagging chain-link fence—they passed beyond what seemed like an unmarked park boundary, the road suddenly swallowed by forest, lined on both sides by towering, densely grown pines and firs.

The two-lane road became a one-lane road with pullouts. The asphalt turned to gravel. Eleanor had the sense they were climbing, gaining elevation, but the unchanging, engulfing woods made it difficult to tell how far they'd come. Occasionally, a mountain range appeared through the clouds, blanketed to the neck in black emerald, peaks of gray rock gouged and scraped as though by massive claws, but most of the time, they were too close to see it, the other mountains occluded by the one they drove upon. She caught a flash of movement in the trees, disturbed branches set bouncing.

They drove up to a swing gate blocking the road. The neon-yellow paint looked simultaneously new and old, vibrant—almost freshly wet—on one end, rust-eaten on the other. Matt left the car idling and his door open as he went to push the gate to the side. When he returned, a curl had fallen from the tight set of his hair. His elegant, thin-soled shoes were thoroughly ruined. "Almost there," he said, out of breath.

The low sedan started to bounce as the texture of the unpaved road worsened. They took a sharp turn into the trees on the right, onto another nameless, signless road that curved almost back the way they'd come, down a steep slope. And all at once, Eleanor could see their destination.

At first glance, she thought it was a logging clear-cut, a vast trapezoid of razed land, cut seemingly arbitrarily out of the forested valley. She didn't understand the scale of the site until they had been driving toward it for a few minutes and it hadn't gotten any larger. The total, surgical annihilation was stunning, an environmentalist's nightmare—the ground scraped clean of the ancient trees and everything that had sheltered within, sterile as salted earth.

She gradually made out the shape of planned streets and plots, space for maybe forty houses along three connected gravel roads. Concrete foundations with rusted twists of steel poking up like weeds. Wood posts, arranged into three-legged pyramids, strung with wire. Puddles that gleamed with oil. Heaps of dirt, open pits. A construction office trailer sat on the far side of the development, backing onto the base of the mountain. Artificial light glowed weakly from within.

Matt's chatter had tapered off, leaving Eleanor to take in the sight in silence. The two plots closest to the construction office, farthest from the mountain road, contained the only completed houses. Bizarrely complete, she thought. The plots were fenced and landscaped, as though they had been dropped from space.

Each a modern, modest two stories with a flat roof, the houses were thoughtful mirrors of each other—pressboard concrete, cedar siding, and broad panels of glass in corresponding locations and proportions. One house had black metal window frames and the other white. They beamed with newness, neat angularity, taste.

Mary had primarily shown Eleanor one-bedroom condos. They'd seen only one single-family home, the shell of a fallen-in structure on a narrow, triangular piece of land, hemmed in by its neighbors with no access to the street. "A fixer-upper," Mary had cheerily declared. "An investment in your future."

Matt parked so the house with white details was enclosed within the passenger-side window, as in a picture frame, cleaved from its surroundings. Eleanor looked at the house. She looked back at Matt, at the barren ground and abandoned sites in the window behind him, the mountain range looming beyond, as though the hills themselves were appalled. She waited for him to speak first.

"The original developer went bankrupt," he said. "The developer who acquired the land is going to resume construction next summer. They don't want to build during the winter. These were the model homes for the original community—to drum up funding from future residents. We're going to look at the one on the right."

Eleanor stepped out. Mud splatter now coated the bottom third of the car, above the base of the doors. "Do you have a car with all-wheel drive?" Matt ventured.

"I have *a* car," Eleanor replied. "It was also my mother's." This, too, Lele had decreed from bed while she was alive, peering over Eleanor's shoulder as she wrote *gift* on the title transfer, the two of them sitting together against the headboard. *Before I go*, she'd said, as though she were only embarking on a trip, a long vacation, somewhere she wouldn't need a car.

A thin, shallow rut marked the edge of the gravel road. Passing the slatted wood fence that ran across the front of the property felt like crossing a fairyland border, the difference stark, like the air itself had changed. Low planters full of native ground cover and ferns—greenery, life!—traced the winding stone path they walked to the front door. Cedar chips filled the gaps between pavers, sending up a warm, woodsy smell with each step to compete with a more subtle but omnipresent odor

Eleanor couldn't quite name—something akin to gasoline or burning plastic.

Matt fiddled with the lockbox on the handle of the front door. He swung the door open and stepped to the side with a dramatic flourish, letting Eleanor enter first. Inside, she inhaled sharply, audibly. She caught the flash of Matt's too-white teeth in her peripheral vision and was dimly annoyed she'd given him the reaction he wanted.

It was as bright inside as outside, floor-to-ceiling windows on every wall, but the light somehow hushed and diffuse, serene, as though she were stepping deeper into the fairyland. The entryway, living room, and dining room were one connected space, sparsely furnished in pieces all made of the same pale blond wood. The two armchairs and wishbone dining chairs had the same wooden skeleton as the entryway bench and dining table.

"Sixteen hundred square feet. Eleven-foot ceilings," Matt said. "The first floor is polished concrete. The second is engineered hardwood."

There was no sofa, nothing on the walls. The rust-red armchair cushions and a large, featureless beige rug were the only suggestions of softness. Even the celestially distant overhead light was made of thin slats of that same wash of wood, arranged into a circular lantern around a glass bowl.

"The staging furniture?" Eleanor asked. Awe had seeped into her voice.

"It's yours if you want it. They're not asking extra for it. Legally they have to remove it all, if you don't." After a pause, Matt added, in the tone of a forced, shameful disclosure, "The previous developer actually built most of the furniture himself. He was a woodworker. He's definitely not coming back for it."

Eleanor sat on the entryway bench to unlace her muddy boots. The surface was smooth and polished under her hand, but the room had an appealing scent of raw wood. Matt offered her a miniature shoehorn he'd drawn from the inner pocket of his suit jacket. She shook her head. He looked pathetic and boyish, waiting in his argyle socks.

A built-in bookcase toward the back blocked their view of the kitchen. A door had been left ajar on the opposite wall. "Powder room and laundry," Matt noted, as they passed.

"There are two bathrooms?" Eleanor said, glancing inside. He grinned again in response.

As they walked into the kitchen, Eleanor was startled by the chaos, after the stark, minimal beauty of the main room. Each of the cabinets was painted a different color—black, white, a dark jasper green, the blue of Matt's suit, unpainted wood, a chocolate stain that let the grain show through—and each door and drawer had different hardware, bars and knobs in different metal finishes, matte black, polished nickel, aged brass, straight lines and curves and curlicues.

"Model home," Matt reminded her.

Eleanor felt an urge to touch everything, to run her hand over the glossy white counter flecked with sparkle, leave the first fingerprints on steel appliances that had never been used. She thought of the last place she'd seen with Mary. The "second bedroom" had turned out to be a narrow alcove off the living room with a bare twin mattress stuffed wall to wall. "This doesn't meet the city's definition of a bedroom, technically," Mary had said. "But it would make a great office!" The carpets had darkened toward the walls, a gradient from dingy off-white to ash black. The wall behind the ancient, yellowing stove had been discolored and mysteriously spongy to the touch. This, Eleanor had thought, is all your mother's life is worth.

Matt let her lead the way upstairs. One bedroom was empty, and the other had a low, wide, simple bed and matching nightstands made of that same pale wood. Both bedrooms had skylights with long, straight light wells. Where the rest of the house was almost overwhelmingly bright and white, the upstairs bathroom was an opulent cave, windowless and tiled to the ceiling in black chevron slate. Small embedded lights over the walk-in shower glittered like stars. She glimpsed herself in the mirror over the floating vanity, and turned quickly away from the greedy, slack-jawed face, its unfamiliar wonder and hope. Incredulous laughter burbled up inside her throat. She pressed her fingertips to her lips to keep them shut.

She drifted to the window at the end of the second-floor corridor, at the top of the stairs, which looked out over the surrounding wasteland, the switchback road on the far hillside they'd driven down. A crow was shredding a scrap of neon-orange tarp in the neighboring plot. It paused to screech, unprompted.

Matt hovered nearby, his hands in his pockets. Eleanor tried to imagine a concrete mixer driving the way they'd come, how the many tons of chunky gravel necessary for the roads had been transported in and how the dozens of old-growth trees had been transported out. Once lush green turned to moon-rock gray, the unfathomable amount of money necessary to carve out this canyon of ugliness and destruction. But inside this house—she felt like she had, her whole adult life, been starved of something that flowed here in abundance.

"How long has this place been on the market?" she asked.

Matt shook his arm out, letting the gaudy watch fall to the end of his wrist. "About twenty minutes."

She stared at him.

"I had some insider information."

As though on cue, she heard the crunch of tires on gravel. She swung back to the window, unconsciously clutching the sill with her fingertips. A sedan much like Matt's was pulling up out front, shiny-topped and wheel wells clotted with mud.

Three other luxury cars crested the hill as she watched, taking the sharp turn one after another.

Matt shifted, standing close behind her and speaking low, as though someone might be listening. "If you want this place, I advise you to make an offer quickly, and to go as high as you're comfortable right away. First and best. If there's a bidding war, you'll lose. As it's a new construction—I can get you all the reports—I also suggest you waive inspection. As is, all in, no contingencies. That's the only way you'll be able to compete. People are going to be coming in with cash."

Mary had never suggested such an aggressive strategy, she thought. But Mary had never succeeded at getting her a home, either. "But I . . . it's . . . I mean, is it even connected to the water and sewer lines? Is there garbage pickup? Is there internet? I need internet to work."

They watched the car below unload, an older woman in a pantsuit and a young, tired-looking couple with a baby. "Water and sewer, yes. Garbage—I'll check, I think that's still being negotiated with the municipality. But the dump isn't too far, if you need to drive it yourself for a little while. The cell coverage here seems decent. You can use that for home internet these days." Matt continued to speak directly into Eleanor's ear from behind, his breath hot on her neck. Not with the intimacy of a lover, but with urgency, discretion, like an aide whispering to the president on TV.

Eleanor looked at the corresponding window on the other house, the mirror image with black frames. It revealed only the blank wall behind it. "Can we see the other one?"

"Only this one is for sale."

"Why?"

"I'm not sure."

The front door opened below, and a chattering female voice rose up the stairwell. "Eleven-foot ceilings," the woman said.

"The first floor is polished concrete. The second is engineered hardwood."

"Eleanor."

She turned to face him. They still stood uncomfortably close together. He held out his hands—the gesture plaintive, or generous, she couldn't tell. An offer or a demand. "You've been around the block. You know what you can get in this price range. You know I'm not going to be able to find you another house that looks remotely like this. If you don't want to live out here, I don't blame you. But if you do, if you'll regret not trying, we need to jump on this now. I'll make a call and start on the paperwork right away."

"I . . . I don't know." But she did know. She wanted it. Her heart had leapt, then hardened, prepared for a fight. This was what Lele would have wanted for her.

2

As soon as Matt dropped her off, before Eleanor had even struggled again with holding open the security door and the inner door of her building on the way in, the morning felt like it had been a dream. She felt certain she wouldn't get the house. She'd been gone for only a couple of hours, not long enough to have made such a momentous decision, the largest purchase of her life. It was like coming home married from a first date. The house itself seemed like something she had imagined, too strange to be real. Twin dream houses standing alone in a valley of death.

She felt a wave of exhaustion as soon as she entered her apartment. She'd been keeping odd hours, waking in time for her clients' appointments and then going back to bed, staying up all night, eating and showering whenever she thought of it. She had no clients scheduled for the rest of the day. She kicked her shoes off and slid into the bed where her mother had died. She napped fitfully.

She woke when her phone pinged by her ear. She had parted from Matt less than an hour ago, but he had already emailed her a raft of documents. His message indicated that he'd been able to work off her previous offers with Mary. *Please review and sign* ASAP *on pp. 3, 6, and 15.*

In the secure folder, there were over a hundred pages—plans and drawings that had been hand-annotated in pen, lien agreements, certifications from subcontractors, scanned legal documents originally in illegible, tiny fonts and worsened in reproduction. She zoomed in and out on her phone, pretending to herself that she understood any of it.

Her mother, ironically, had been a loan officer at the same regional bank for thirty years. Lele had been frugal and shrewd, had paid for Eleanor's prolonged education in full, sold her own paid-off house to pay for her medical expenses at the end. Eleanor had had every opportunity to learn from her, but money had always bored and frightened her—despite Lele's best efforts, all Eleanor retained was a hazy, anxious idea of money as a scarce, essential resource, as though she were responsible for generating the oxygen in the air she breathed, and she could die at any moment from lack of effort. When she'd shared a practice and an office—with her mentor, Teddy, the psychologist who'd first supervised her licensing hours—Lele had kept the books for her, had negotiated with insurance companies, told her which clients were behind, even pretended to be Eleanor on the phone when necessary. Money was her mother's domain. Eleanor would rather not look, not know, and as long as she'd had Lele, she'd never had to. Now she took appointments through a third-party service owned by a tech company. They deposited money into her account that vaguely aligned with how many clients she saw, and she didn't question it.

She signed on pages three, six, and fifteen on her phone, three taps of her thumb, nestled under the bedcovers. It still felt unreal, the house a thing so obviously beyond her grasp. Eleanor's fourth failed offer had been on a sunny, closet-sized studio in the desirable north end of the city. She'd felt the natural light and location outweighed the fact that she could reach both the refrigerator and the toilet from the bed. Ten other buyers had agreed.

Her phone pinged twice immediately: an acknowledgment email, and a text from her former colleague and office mate, whom she had in her phone as *Dr. Teddy*. She had not heard from him in over three years.

E, it's been ages! Did you know they're demolishing our old building? I just passed by and thought of you. Drink tonight to mourn?

She felt a chill at his phrasing. To mourn. She pulled the covers up to her chin. He didn't know. Teddy's was a world where her mother was still alive.

• • •

Eleanor and Teddy met at a bar near their former office, where they'd gone a few times when they worked together. The area was quieter than she remembered, the streets empty, neighboring storefronts shuttered. The bar's front windows were boarded up, a mural of flowers painted across the nailed sheets of plywood, the words STILL OPEN! integrated into the design.

Inside, the few patrons were scattered across the room, as though sitting as far from one another as possible. An unfamiliar man at the bar looked up when she walked in. His heathered gray polo strained against the bulk of his body, the fabric darkened with sweat, a salt stain visible on the underside of his baseball cap. The stranger stared at Eleanor with frank, open hostility. She didn't know for which facet of her identity he hated her on sight—which villain she resembled to him, what fantasy he projected.

"E, over here!"

Teddy waved from a table against the wall. As she joined him, he waved in another direction. The bartender sighed, walked the long way around the bar and over to their table. Teddy turned back to Eleanor. "What are you having?"

She tried to think of a drink that sounded grown-up, and then chastised herself for the thought. She *was* a grown-up. And why should she care what Teddy thought, anyway? Trying to impress him was an old, useless habit. He had a wineglass in front of him, down to its purple dregs. "What are you drinking?" she asked.

"The pinot noir. It's not bad at all. Shall we get a bottle? Do you want anything to eat?"

"Kitchen's closed," the bartender said. Her labret piercing gave her a slight lisp. "Everyone's out sick. I'm the only one working tonight. I can bring you some nuts and olives, if you want."

"Please," Teddy said. "And a bottle of the pinot, and another glass." He waited for the bartender to leave before adding, "I'm relieved to learn you still drink. I was just at a conference, and I swear, no one in your generation drinks anymore. The other old fogies and I were the only ones getting real drinks. The younger attendees were all ordering mocktails and kombucha and leaving the hotel bar by ten. They weren't even alcoholics! Alcoholics at least have fun stories."

Eleanor laughed politely. The bartender returned, put down small dishes of nuts and olives, popped the wine cork. She was pouring hurriedly into Teddy's glass, the wine glugging, when he interrupted her. "Aren't you going to let me taste it first?"

"You already had a glass. It's the same wine."

"But that was a different bottle. How do I know this one isn't skunked?"

Her mouth tightened, her pierced lower lip jutting out. Her eyes shone with murder. "Go on and taste it, then."

Teddy swished, breathed in, took a delicate sip. The bartender met Eleanor's eye, and she tried to smile in a noncommittal way, neither endorsing nor denouncing Teddy's behavior. "This will do," he said.

The bartender plunked down the bottle on the table and walked away. Teddy picked it up and filled both of their glasses. "She doesn't seem especially concerned about her tip," he sniffed.

Eleanor studied Teddy. He looked exactly as he had when she'd seen him last, the same deep tan and wispy white hair, while she felt she had aged a thousand years. The wine was tart and astringent and intense; she hardly ever drank anymore. "How have you been, Teddy?"

"Oh, good, good. Better lately. It was a hard couple of years, of course. As it was for everyone. Are you back to seeing patients in person?"

"No, I've stuck to virtual."

"Really? I couldn't stand it. Sitting at a computer all day, staring at the tops of people's heads in those little boxes. Their voices stuttering as the connection died." Teddy dug a slippery olive out of the dish with his bare fingers, tossed it into his mouth. She could see the green flesh squish as he bit down, like popping an eyeball. "And then the *masks*. Here we are, trying to build this delicate, healing relationship, with all these barriers between us." He sucked on his teeth, savoring the flavor.

Eleanor could feel the wine after only a few mouthfuls—an unpleasant heat in her face and gut, a trailing blur when she turned her head. She named the online platform she used. "Their video client is a little more reliable, I've found."

"Oh, I've been hearing a lot about that one. Do you like it?"

She shrugged. "They take care of all the administrative stuff. I don't make very much per billing hour, but I have basically no expenses or overhead, either. It's a lot of first-time clients, though. Introductory sessions. Most people don't come back after the first few."

"Of course they don't." Teddy threw back more olives, munching wetly. He pointed at her for emphasis, his fingertip slick with olive juice and saliva. "Because it's not *real*."

She took a long drink. "I do a lot of referring them to other apps."

Teddy topped up her glass, leaving greasy fingerprints on the label of the bottle. "I have no idea what that means."

"There's a good one for CBT. They keep sending me free access codes to give out. It has worksheets, trackers, weekly assignments. It's perfect for that kind of client, the ones who want homework we can go over together. There are also ones for sleep and meditation. Prescriptions, of course."

"Why wouldn't you just send them to their physician?"

"Most of them don't have a PCP. They just fill out a little questionnaire and the drugs come to their door. I have an affiliate discount code."

"That's legal?"

"There's a doctor involved somewhere."

Teddy shook his head. "Have you given any more thought to going back to get your PhD? Or medical school? It would open a lot of doors. A master's in psychology is—well, not *worthless*, but . . ."

Eleanor glanced at the glass in her hand, surprised to find it half empty again.

He rooted around in the mixed nuts, selecting individual peanuts. "I know there was all that unpleasantness with Michael—Dr. Culver, rather. I understand why you exited your combined program the way you did. He wasn't the most enlightened fellow, but not every supervisor will be like that. And he did connect us, right? So it wasn't all bad."

The man at the bar was watching her again, with that same focused, personal resentment, glowering in the shadow of his ball cap. Her eye had instinctively gone to him at the mention of Dr. Culver. He sat with his knees wide on the barstool, turned toward her, the cracked green leather visible between his thighs. *It wasn't all bad*, her brain echoed. The man smacked his lips, and for a moment, she thought he was mouthing a word in her direction. *Liar*, maybe. Or *killer*.

Teddy licked the salt from his fingers. "I have connections at a number of schools around the country, if you want me to refer you. In the most glowing terms, of course."

Teddy meant well, she thought. He always meant well. What version did Teddy believe, that allowed him to be professionally cordial with Dr. Culver while remaining Eleanor's mentor and friend? That some abstract *unpleasantness* had occurred between them, something distasteful that was better left unsaid. Dr. Culver at fault for being *unenlightened*, brutish, old-fashioned, in a way that had little bearing on him as a scientist. And it was all so long ago, now. She rubbed the side of her jaw, trying to relax the muscle. A nerve in her neck jumped. The stranger turned back to his beer.

"That's very generous," she said, keeping her tone light. "But I don't think so. I've been out of school for nine years now. I wouldn't know how to do it anymore."

"Nine years? It can't have been that long."

She tried to give a level stare. Her spine swayed.

"But you're so young," he said.

"I'm really not, Teddy."

He returned her gaze for a long, thoughtful moment. "I think I tell myself that you're young because that means I'm not so terribly old."

"Not *terribly* old."

"Ha-ha," he deadpanned. He topped up their glasses again. "My, we are moving quickly through this bottle." He looked past her, toward the boarded-up windows, the direction in which their old building lay silent and gutted. "I can't even remember what was in all those tiny offices other than ours. Can you?"

"Hmm, let's see. There was a dentist on our floor. At least two dentists—one orthodontic surgeon. There was an accounting firm on the floor below us, and several lawyers, an architecture group, that woman who sewed costumes. There was a dance studio somewhere—I remember seeing kids in ballet tights on the stairs. The ground floor had a coffee shop and a dog groomer."

"Impressive. I do remember the coffee shop." Teddy leaned forward. She could see the peanut skins and bits of olive stuck in his teeth. "I keep thinking, what happened to all of those people? Where did they go?"

"They went wherever it is we went," Eleanor said.

Her phone dinged in her pocket. Her eyes flicked down toward it. Teddy leaned back, looking disappointed. "I'm going to use the little boys' room," he said, pushing away from the table.

The small text on her screen swam before her. She struggled to focus her eyes. Another email with a secure link from Matt. *OK to go ahead on your behalf? Initial on pp. 1 and 2, sign on p. 3.* She signed digitally without reading. Why was Matt still working? Surely houses weren't bought and sold on a phone, in a bar, at nine p.m. on a Sunday.

She readied herself to tell Teddy about the house when he returned from the bathroom, planning how to phrase the story to make it as entertaining as possible, but as soon as he sat back down, he asked, "How's your mother doing?"

She heard herself answer from a distance, as though it were the voice of someone else. "She passed away last year."

"Oh my god. I'm so sorry, E. Was it COVID?"

"Cancer."

"How old was she?"

"Sixty-one."

Teddy closed his eyes, his hand on his chest, as though wounded by her answer. Eleanor didn't know Teddy's precise age, but sixty-one was likely well behind him. "God, that's so young. How are you holding up? I know you were extremely close."

Eleanor managed a thin, watery smile. "We were. She was the only person I saw during lockdown."

"Were you able to be with her when she passed?"

"Yes. She actually moved in with me, for—for what turned out to be the last couple months."

"You were taking care of her on your own? I watched Mira go through that with her parents. It was just dreadful."

"Mostly. My mom had a cousin who was a retired nurse. She helped out a little. But they didn't get along, so she stopped coming around eventually."

"That's unfortunate. These things can bring out the worst in people."

"It wasn't like that." Eleanor paused to choose her words. "Mom's meds were really complicated. She had all these alarms on her phone and a notebook by the bed, where she wrote down everything she took, to keep it straight. Cece—her cousin—kept saying my mom was confused, was making mistakes, when she wasn't. She was completely lucid until the very end. I think Cece was also in denial. When Mom was first diagnosed, the oncologist gave her good odds for two to five years with treatment, maybe more, but she was gone in six months. And the whole time, Cece just refused to accept what was happening in front of us. She kept pointing to the initial prognosis, like it was gospel. 'He said two to five years!' And there's nothing my mom hated more than false hope."

Teddy twisted the stem of his glass, like he didn't know what to say. "I remember you used to make dinner for her every Sunday," he said, trying for a segue. "I always thought that was so sweet."

Her mouth felt dry. She drained her glass. The man at the bar was gone. She hadn't noticed him leaving. She hadn't been keeping track of him, as she should have. He could be waiting for her outside. He could be in any darkened doorway, around any corner she passed on the way home. "I never cooked her dinner."

"Oh? I could have sworn you—"

"She *brought over* dinner every Sunday. She came in the afternoon and cleaned my apartment and did my laundry. She came on Sundays because Monday was garbage day."

Teddy's face looked carefully arranged, a neutral mask. "She . . . took out the trash for you? Every week?"

"Yes. She also managed my money. All of my bank accounts were joint, in her name."

He continued to show no reaction. "And how did you feel about that?"

Eleanor laughed once, like a hiccup, high-pitched. "I loved it. I loved it!" Her voice broke on the second *it*. "I dated this guy, Antoni, whose fiancée had left him for being too much of a mama's boy, because his mom was too involved in their lives. And even he thought Mom and I were too much. He wanted some weekends to ourselves, thought I was too dependent on her. The irony being that *he* lived with his mother! A total hypocrite."

"I remember Antoni. You seemed very fond of him. You didn't resent her, after that? Even a little bit?"

She shook her head. The room streaked around her. "Not at all. I just wish she was still here, to tell me what to do. I constantly wish I could ask her for advice. I feel like a child, in the worst possible way. Like I'm five years old and she abandoned me in a parking lot. Sometimes I'll be talking to someone, a bank teller or a waiter or a canvasser on the street, and I'll have this moment of genuine dissociation and confusion, like, why are they talking to me like this? Can't they see I'm only a child?"

He nodded. "Regression is a common response to losing a parent."

"Don't start with that shit, Teddy."

He held up his hands in a *mea culpa* gesture. "I know what you mean, though. Mira started up her supper club again, and sometimes I'll look around the table and think, Who are all these geezers? What have they done with my beautiful friends, my beautiful wife? I look in the mirror and expect to see myself at seventeen, at twenty-five, at forty. And instead this old man stares back, older than my father when he died, someone who couldn't possibly be me."

"You look great."

"Thank you. Please keep lying to me."

Soon afterward, the bartender appeared by their table, holding a card reader. "We're closing up soon," she said. "Last call." Eleanor looked around and realized they were the only customers left.

"It's only ten," Teddy said.

The bartender shrugged.

"Two old-fashioneds, then," he said.

"Are you serious?"

"You said 'last call.'"

The bartender rolled her eyes as she stalked back to the bar.

"She's going to spit in those drinks," Eleanor said.

"It's ten o'clock!" Teddy cried again. "What's wrong with this town?"

They downed their cocktails quickly, presumptive spit and all. Teddy asked for the check to be split. Eleanor grimaced. She never would have chosen such an expensive wine, or ordered a final round out of spite. She felt queasy, an acid taste at the back of her tongue.

They waited together on the sidewalk out front. They gazed down the block at their old building, pockmarked by broken windows, wrapped in temporary construction fencing. "Do you think it's haunted?" Teddy asked.

"By what?"

"Dentists, lawyers. Little ballerinas. Us," he said, "as we used to be."

His rideshare arrived first. As they watched the car idle at a red light a block away, she let Teddy embrace her. He kissed her forehead, his lips papery and dry. "Let's not go another three years this time," he said.

When he lingered there, the wine and bourbon strong on his breath, she pushed him back gently. "Go home to your wife, Teddy."

He climbed into the car with a bleary wave. Nothing had ever happened between them, nothing she couldn't ignore or deny. That had been the trouble with Dr. Culver, ultimately. He wouldn't let her pretend not to know what he wanted.

3

Eleanor woke to her ringing phone. She was clutching it in her fist in her sleep, her hand tucked under her pillow, under her head. Her neck and shoulder ached on that side. She rolled onto her back, pulling the phone close enough to see. Matt was calling, it was just after seven a.m., and her battery was almost dead.

The phone slipped from her grip, smacking her in the face. She fumbled to grab it and answer the call, checking her nose for tenderness with the other hand. "Hello?"

"Eleanor! I have great news. We got it!"

"We got . . . what?"

"The house! The seller accepted your offer."

She sat bolt upright. Her hangover asserted itself.

"So, look, you'll need to transfer the earnest money today. If you want to avoid wire fees, we can meet up at your bank and you can give me a cashier's check, and I'll run it over."

"Wait—when did this happen? You already submitted the offer?"

"What do you mean? They got four offers last night, including ours. They reviewed this morning, and you won. I told you no contingencies was the way to go."

"This morning?" She checked the time again, the faint beginnings of sunrise in the window.

"I waited to call. I didn't want to wake you."

"I—I have client appointments this morning."

"That's fine," he said. "It just has to be by end of day. We also have to meet up with Vance. He said anytime after two p.m. will be fine."

"Who?"

"The mortgage broker you and Mary were working with."

"Oh, right." When Eleanor tried to remember what Vance looked like, she just saw Matt again, pictured the same tie-less suit and Cheshire grin, only seated behind a desk. "Vance knows about the sale already? When did you talk to him?"

"This morning," Matt said, patiently. "Do you want me to pick you up, or should I just meet you at the bank?"

"I—I can meet you." She heard Lele's voice in her head: *Take a breath. Think before you speak.* "Can you remind me, how much—"

"Ten thousand," Matt said.

"Oh."

After a beat, he said, "Can you not access ten thousand right away?"

She had left the entirety of her inheritance in her checking account, trying to pretend it didn't exist. She inhaled and exhaled slowly. "I can."

"Great. One thirty okay? And then we'll go straight to Vance?"

She wished, suddenly, that she had brought Teddy home with her, even with everything that would mean. At least she would have woken up with him here, with an adult in the room.

• • •

The worst part, it turned out, was the fifteen minutes Eleanor spent standing outside the bank, waiting for Matt, her hands and face raw and chapped in the icy wind, early for October. She rubbed the edge of the check in her pocket, feeling a strange wash of dread. She pictured the check getting blown out of her hand and washing down the rain gutter. She pictured taking her hand out of her pocket and finding some other, meaningless scrap of paper, the check inexplicably gone. A man in a long coat stopped to ask her for the time, and she felt certain he knew, that this was a pretext to rob her.

She found herself thinking about the night Lele died. That evening, Lele had insisted Eleanor wash her hair for her in the sink, leaning her head back over the edge of a chair. Though Lele had refused conventional chemotherapy, her hair seemed thinner, and had gone completely gray, where only months ago the black had been scarcely streaked with scattered silver, like tinsel. Eleanor poured cupped handfuls of water over visible strips of scalp. Lele shuddered and winced the whole time, as though each hair follicle were an open wound, the skin waxy and pink. She wouldn't let Eleanor stop. Eleanor dried her mother's hair as delicately as she could, then helped her back into bed, easing her head onto a towel-covered pillow.

Eleanor had lain beside her in the dark, holding her hand under the covers. All night, she listened to the time between Lele's breaths lengthen. Lele smelled like herself, like the hand cream and shampoo she'd used for as long as Eleanor could remember, floral and faintly medicinal, but the smell seemed to concentrate and intensify as the night wore on, to fill the room like a fog. Sometime in the small hours of the morning, Lele inhaled a ragged, stuttering breath, like a child trying not to cry, and did not exhale.

Eleanor didn't move, didn't check. She stayed holding her mother's warm, supple hand until daylight had arrived in full, the sun first limning Lele's edges—the tip of her nose, the piped collar of her pajama top, the peak her toes made under the duvet—before growing blinding, confrontational, undeniable.

Per Lele's instructions, Eleanor tried to disconnect the smoke detector. As she unscrewed it from the ceiling mount, it started chirping, almost jolting her off the stepladder. The sound was earsplitting at close range as she strained overhead to unplug the hardwired connector, a plastic tongue-in-groove casing over the wires in the ceiling. Once it clicked free, the bottom half of the alarm fell into her hands, continuing to screech. Still teetering on the ladder, she found the backup battery in the back and used her nail to pop it out. The chirping finally ceased.

She tried burning the medication notebook in the sink with the long-handled lighter she used for candles. The fire wouldn't take. Flameless, stinking black smoke rose in its stead, the notebook wicking up the moisture left around the drain by the leaky tap.

She eventually ripped the wet, blackened mush of pages from the spine and flushed them down the toilet, then stuffed the cardboard cover in the trash. She arranged the pill bottles on the kitchen counter, beside Lele's neatly stacked DNR and will. Eleanor would, eventually, call the palliative care unit of the last hospital where Lele had been treated, instead of 911, just as Lele had told her to, and say the words Lele had made her repeat: *It was expected and is not an emergency.* She had a vivid memory of standing by her childhood front door with Lele, at four years old, reciting her name, her mother's name, and their address, to prove she knew it by heart, that moment blurring with this one.

But first, before she called anyone, she closed her bedroom door and sat heavily on the living room couch, stared at her slumped reflection in the blank, black screen of the television. She was reluctant to bring other people into the apartment, to relinquish her mother's body. As long as Eleanor sat there, her mother could be sleeping in the next room, and no one would take her away. She let an hour go by this way, then another, the sun passing to the other side of the sky. When they did come, and then when she was alone again, her instinct was to debrief with Lele, to tell her that all her planning turned out to be unnecessary. *I did everything right, but no one cared, Mom. No one was paying attention.*

The check felt unnervingly flimsy. She wanted to give Matt a bar of gold bullion, something with heft. Or better, the weight of a corpse. When he arrived, he shook her hand in congratulations, and her memories nested telescopically before her: Handing the check to Matt felt like watching her mother die, which felt like rehearsing for her first day of preschool. *My name is Eleanor Fan. My mother is Lele Fan. I live at 3588 King Street, unit 201. It was expected and is not an emergency.*

4

Eleanor took the road through Bering Rock slower than Matt had, this time trying to note each business, acquaint herself with her new town. The diner, the drive-through espresso hut, the gas station. Laundromat, motel, barber, Chinese restaurant. A dead movie theater with a marquee that read THANK YOU FOR 25 YEARS! A church that looked like a small house, save for the bell in an open dormer on the roof. A former Mexican restaurant, now for lease, the sign bleached of its greens and reds.

The weather was fickle—cottony clouds, sun showers materializing and disappearing, evaporating too fast for her windshield wipers, warmer than it had been in weeks. After the road narrowed and the asphalt ended, Lele's ten-year-old, bubble-shaped hatchback continued to handle just fine, rattling steadily along.

She pulled up to the neon-painted swing gate and hopped out to push it open. The rusted end left a residue on her hands, an iron-colored smudge.

Eleanor inched around the tight final bend. The development land looked even more surreal than she remembered.

The harshness of its borders, straight lines cut into the forest, made the trees at the edges look like furious sentries, standing shoulder to shoulder, forming an infantry wall. There were patches of regrowth she hadn't noticed before, crusty yellow lichen in the abandoned homesites, stray tufts of wild grass. Like the Earth was the dome of a human head, and this patch of sunken, denuded, discolored land was record of some terrible injury.

But the two houses, one now hers, still existed in their own separate, storybook domain, under the watchful eye of the construction office set slightly higher on the rise behind. The light was again on inside.

She had thought she would get to meet someone from the company that owned the land, but everything had happened either electronically or through Matt. He'd seemed proud of the rapid closing date—within the month—though that wasn't something she could recall asking for. He had been the one to present her with the key. They'd met up in a Starbucks the day before, and he jingled it at her as she walked in, as though entertaining a baby. She had three months left on her lease, and as much of a strain as it was to carry both her rent and the new mortgage, she hated the thought of leaving the apartment behind. To surrender the walls that held the memory of Lele's presence, on top of everything else.

She was relieved to find she still loved the house, seeing it for only the second time. Backgrounded by the forested mountains, it looked incongruously man-made but beautiful, like a large-scale public art piece. As a housewarming gift, Matt had bought and had delivered a bear-proof metal shed, about the size of a child's playhouse, for storing her garbage between runs to the dump. It blended into the side of the house.

She had not attached the key to her key chain, had kept it on its separate ring in her pocket. It had the feel of something borrowed in hand. The key stuck on her first attempt at putting it into the lock, needing to be eased in with a certain finesse. Like the house didn't trust her, resisted her entrance.

She had opted to keep all the severe wood furniture. As she walked inside, she wished she could leave the house just as it was. Keep the surfaces clear, the drawers and shelves empty. Retain this monastic spaciousness and peace. Even just her coat, tossed onto the bench, felt like a sunburst of mess.

Her old apartment was full of Lele's things. After Lele had sold her house, she'd been ruthless and unsentimental in discarding her furniture and possessions, but the fraction she'd kept still overflowed from the closets and cabinets, boxes stacked high in the corners. The small, threadbare towels she'd preferred, finding Eleanor's bath sheets to be a mildewy extravagance. A lifetime supply of the instant coffee that Eleanor thought tasted like burning tires. Obscure kitchen tools that Eleanor had never and would never use. Colorful plastic step stools tucked under every shelf and counter, as Lele had been just under five feet tall. The bulky engraved clock the bank gave Lele when she was forcibly retired, her full legal name misspelled.

After Lele was diagnosed, she'd requested medical leave from her branch manager. A few days later, she received an email from someone at the main branch congratulating her on her retirement. When she went back to her manager, he looked at the forwarded email and said, evenly, "There must have been a misunderstanding. But you've considered just retiring, haven't you? You're only a year or two away anyway. Maybe this is a sign that it's the right time."

The day the clock arrived, Lele showed up at Eleanor's unannounced, holding the heavy package in her arms. She lay in Eleanor's bed all day. Eleanor didn't understand what had happened, exactly, beyond that her mother wanted to keep working and wouldn't be. She opened the box and found a retirement card from Lele's former coworkers, who had not come to a consensus on whether to mention her cancer—*I know you'll beat this thing* was scrawled alongside *Best wishes on this new chapter!*

Since her drink with Teddy, Eleanor had been thinking about her ex-boyfriend Antoni again. She had an irrational conviction that, in the years they'd been apart, his mother had died as well. And if they met again, as motherless people, it would be like they were reborn, remade as strangers. Vulnerable in a new way, like seeing each other naked for the first time.

• • •

She intended to move in slowly, one carload at a time. She'd spent the night packing. How little was hers, as opposed to Lele's, was highlighted by the way the space in the small car had felt infinite. With the back seats folded down, she had first placed a suitcase of essentials—her toothbrush, some socks and underwear—and ended up bringing almost her entire wardrobe, all her towels and linens, everything in the kitchen and bathroom she actually used. Her life compressed down to shockingly few boxes.

One by one, she carried the boxes inside to their corresponding rooms but didn't unpack them. Her top priority, that first day, was to set up the internet, as she had clients in the afternoon. Matt had been right about using the cell network for home internet, and it was mercifully simple, a black tower the size of a shoebox that she could install herself.

Without a desk, she sat at her new dining table. A pop-up on the therapy platform noted her weaker connection, and recommended she change her settings to preference audio and downgrade the video quality. The effect of these changes was eerie, her client's face smudging when her head moved, her features muddled, her patterned top swirling of its own accord. The room behind her was rendered papyrus-colored, blocky, and depthless, like a cubist pencil drawing.

"Good afternoon, Kristy," Eleanor said. "How are you today?"

"I'm good. Great. Really great."

"I'm glad to hear that."

They'd been working together for three months, but Kristy's face now seemed changed in low resolution. She wore her hair pulled back from the crown, in a high ponytail or bun, and the blond melded into the skin, making her appear bald and large-headed, pale and ovoid as a boiled egg. A stripe of pink across her nose and cheeks could have been anything, in real life—a cheerful flush, makeup, acne, rosacea—but appeared on camera as stark as the strawberry segment in Neapolitan ice cream.

"I found this support group for shopping addicts. It's helping me a lot." Kristy had a distinctive voice, trilling and breathless, with a quick, frantic way of speaking that was not quite a stutter. The new settings made her sound slightly compressed and robotic, like an artificial replica of a voice Eleanor thought she knew well.

"You found this group in the last week? Do they meet in person or online?"

"Online. Well, they don't really have meetings. It's more like a forum."

Eleanor waited for Kristy's smeared head to resolve. She briefly resembled a cartoon alien, her dark eyes expanding with the distortion; then the rest of her face caught up, making her eyes disappear altogether, a contiguous blur of flesh from temple to temple. "I'm glad to hear you've found it helpful." Hadn't Eleanor said she was glad once already? She must sound insincere. It was distracting, hypnotic, watching the visual echoes of Kristy's head—repeating, expanding shadows appearing each time she moved.

"Yeah. For one thing, I'm not nearly as bad as most of the people who post."

"I'm sorry—is the video quality bothering you?"

Kristy snapped back into herself as the picture cleared. "What do you mean? It looks fine to me."

"Never mind. Go on. What was helpful about the forum?"

"Okay, so, this is the most important part—people on the forum make rules. They write lists of rules for themselves so they won't shop as much, and post the lists. And I was so inspired by this. So I made my own list."

She had the energy of a child eager to show a drawing they'd made. Eleanor obliged. "What are your rules?"

"Okay. Rule number one: When I want something, instead of buying it right away, I put it on a wish list, where it has to stay for two weeks before I buy it. Rule number two: I only buy stuff in person, since my worst shopping happens online. Rule number three: I bought this little calendar and a pack of stickers, and for each day I don't spend any money, I put a sticker on that day."

"These sound very reasonable," Eleanor said. The video froze briefly, Kristy's irises overlaid with rectangles of turquoise light. Eleanor looked at her notes, which she had up in a second window. "Did any packages arrive this week?"

Eleanor could see Kristy's shoulders drop, even as she was a blurry silhouette, eyed and then eyeless. Eleanor was getting used to the erratic image.

"Yeah," Kristy said. "A few."

"What's a few?"

"I don't know. Like, three. More than three. Seven? A bunch. I don't know."

"Have you opened them? Are you enjoying your new things? Did you return anything you didn't like?" They had agreed, in an earlier session, that Eleanor would ask Kristy these questions every week.

"I haven't opened them yet."

"Why do you think you haven't opened them?"

Kristy was shifting around, worsening the effect. She seemed almost to disappear and reappear, the video predictively infilling the beige background, guessing at her absence. "I've been busy. Anyway, a lot of them were final sale. I can't return them."

"What did you buy this week, besides the calendar and the stickers?"

"Not much. I only bought stuff one other time."

"What was it?"

Kristy sighed. "A makeup organizer. A pair of boots and a jacket. Some basic shirts. Some candles. A new foundation. They were on sale."

"When did you buy them?"

"I placed the order on Tuesday."

"Did anything out of the ordinary happen on Tuesday?"

"No, not really. My boss was . . . she kind of yelled at me in front of everyone. Over something that wasn't even my fault. But she's always yelling at me. I wouldn't call it out of the ordinary."

"I'm sorry you were treated that way. What did you do right after she yelled at you?"

"I went to the bathroom and cried."

"And you did some shopping that evening?"

Kristy took so long to answer that Eleanor thought the call had dropped. She had become a gray, pixelated snowman shape, merging again with the room. "No. I bought that stuff right then. In the bathroom at work, on my phone."

Eleanor waited, but the picture remained fractured and unreal. "Are you still considering looking for another job?"

"You say that like it's easy. Do you know what it's like out there? I need this job. To pay down the debt, like we talked about."

"Okay, let's put a pin in that for now. What about talking to Lee? About the credit cards? Last week, you mentioned you would feel better if he knew." Eleanor wouldn't usually push this hard, not with Kristy. Kristy liked to be in control of their sessions, to therapize herself, and Eleanor didn't find it productive to stand in her way, when she was generally moving, however slowly, toward the right conclusions. But today Eleanor felt an inexplicable urgency, a sense that she was losing Kristy as her image faded in and out.

Kristy exhaled heavily, blowing out the mic. "No, because now I have these rules! So I'll be able to pay them off and Lee never has to know." Her voice became pinched. "I feel like you're not listening. You're just reading your notes at me. Where are you, anyway? You're somewhere different than you usually are."

Eleanor had assumed her backdrop was as indistinct and abstracted to Kristy as Kristy's was to her. "I'm sorry I made you feel unheard. And yes, I moved recently." After a pause, she added, "I bought a house."

Even as she said it, she wished she hadn't. Kristy's mounting debt loomed between them, as palpable as a third person.

The video sharpened. Kristy's ordinary face in its full, detailed glory, down to the smallest, aching movements of her brow. "Congratulations," she said, deflated.

• • •

Sunset came on early, the valley surrounded by mountains and rises on all sides, the sun dropping behind the western hills during Eleanor's last appointment. She turned on the canned downlights and the wooden chandelier, and the room became almost painfully, clinically bright. It was only then that she realized the house had no window coverings. She had somehow not thought about it all day, or noticed during that first tour—she'd just admired the large windows, the dramatic flood of daylight. In a way, it wouldn't matter for a long time. There'd be no one to see her until next summer, when Matt had said construction would resume, and the days were only getting shorter, so waking with the sun wouldn't be an issue.

She turned off the downlights. From one of the front windows, she noted that the other house, the black-frame house, did have a mix of curtains and roller shades, some open and some closed. All the windows were dark. She would have to worry about whoever lived there looking in, if in fact someone did live there. There were no other cars.

She turned off the chandelier, plunging the room back into darkness. She walked around the perimeter, window to window. She couldn't make out much in any direction. The distant, tightly packed trees were black in the darkness, as were the empty building sites. Only the gravel road reflected the moonlight. The light in the construction office cut a small square of yellow into the blackened mountainside, but seemed to cast no outward glow.

An animal fear rose in her, a sense of being exposed, surrounded, seen and unseeing. She wanted to feel celebratory and adult, her first night in the first home she'd ever owned, but she couldn't help picturing the house from the outside, her figure visible as she walked from room to room, as she sat at the table, climbed the stairs, got into bed.

She tested the taps and flushed the toilets. She felt amazed everything worked, everything was real. She could not bring herself to strip completely to shower, even though the upstairs bathroom had no windows.

The air in the bedroom felt stale. The mechanism to open the window was complex: a flip lock on either side, a winch in the middle she had to turn to send the top half of the window outward and up, like a hat brim. That noxious industrial smell of the surrounding land entered the room, but it came with a breeze, carrying the scent of waxy pine needles and turned earth from farther upwind.

She made up the bed with the clean sheets she'd brought. She smoothed and tucked the bedding crisply. All of this belonged to her. All these bare, lovely rooms, more than she'd ever thought possible. Lele would be proud. She would be relieved to know that Eleanor had broken through the inertial tide that had carried her along since Lele's death, that she had done something so drastic, invested wisely, transformed loss into safety and power.

In her new house, Eleanor told herself, she would stop staying up all night, stop sleeping between clients in the middle of the day, stop drinking so much coffee she could feel her heart vibrating in her throat like a live bird. She would eat regular meals, take her own therapeutic advice, rejoin the land of the living. Here, she would choose what to remember and what to forget.

• • •

Rain pattering on the skylight woke her in the night. She got up and closed the window, fumbling to remember how in the dark, which way to wind the handle, unsure if the locks had caught their latches.

She felt her way back into the bed. She looked up at the skylight, droplets striking the glass and forming ripples and dimples, lulling her with their gentle drumbeat.

A hand slipped into Eleanor's under the duvet.

Small, bony. Callused fingers, but preternaturally soft along the thin skin of the back, from the hand cream Lele had kept in her purse and beside every sink, applied a dozen times a day.

Lele lay beside her, flat on her back. She wore the cotton pajamas she'd died in, buttoned to the collar and densely patterned with orange flowers, each bloom the size of a fingernail. Her grip was loose and limp. Lele turned just her head toward Eleanor, smiling—a mischievous, impish grin she'd never worn in life.

In the first months after Lele died, Eleanor had of course seen her everywhere: in a stranger's gait as they walked down the sidewalk, in the slant of their shoulders, the back of any dark head of hair. Any woman with her coloring, her height, or any single shared feature—her rounded nose in profile, her unpierced ears, a coat she might have worn—had entered Eleanor's field of vision as Lele. Before the turn, as in a magic trick, before the betrayal that revealed they had been someone else all along. But never like this, never a sustained visitation in her bed—a Lele that stayed, a Lele she could touch.

The smile on her face ground against Eleanor's memories like an ill-fitting gear.

You're not my mother, she thought, the knowledge immediate, reflexive. But of course it wasn't. It was a pleasant, lucid-feeling dream, something Eleanor had made for herself. A housewarming gift from her own mind.

5

The rain, in the morning, had turned violent, now crashing upon the skylights as though trying to break through. Wind drove the water sideways, lashing against the windows. The warping streams made it appear as though the house were underwater. Eleanor had woken late, in the murky aquarium light. She had a client in less than half an hour.

She was alone.

As she stepped out of bed, Eleanor's bare feet landed in a puddle.

Water was pooling beneath the bedroom window she'd opened the night before. A thin stream of water ran down the inside of the glass. She must not have closed it fully.

She unlocked and opened the window. Water gushed in and onto her pajamas and feet, from where it had pooled along the top of the frame. She winched it closed as tightly as she could. When she depressed the locks, they felt softer than before, and didn't click.

She had left the moving box containing towels on the upstairs landing. She tore the tape open with her hands, grabbed one, and used it to sop up the puddle as best she could. Over her wet pajamas, she threw on one of her rotation of solid-colored sweaters that were presentable from the chest up.

She rushed downstairs, leaving wet footprints. The wind was rattling the windows, and a louder, metallic rattling, like a propeller on a loose bolt, was coming from the kitchen. She sat down at her computer, the other chairs tucked in around the dining table, hurriedly pulling her hair into a bun as the platform loaded.

Her client appeared on-screen. Choppy when in motion, edges and borders softened. He talked, as he had for the last four sessions, about his more accomplished older brother. "Let's revisit some of our strategies for dealing with envy," Eleanor said.

She leaned forward as she answered the session-end prompts, the font small and unscalable, her face six inches from the screen. When she sat back, closing the laptop lid, her eyes darted left, drawn to a change, something out of place.

Lele sat in the chair at the head of the table. She was dressed in the same orange pajamas, smiling again, but now her mouth was stretched tight, her eyes blank, as though she'd been posing too long for a photograph. For a photographer who would neither take the picture nor let her go.

• • •

Eleanor's focus in grad school was in agent-based computer simulation, which had been briefly in vogue, Dr. Culver a leader in the field. In grandiose moods, in the basement bar where grad students gathered, Eleanor described their work as simulating possible histories of mankind, scientifically testing theories of human nature—what simple drives led to the complex emergent outcomes of culture and society. In practice, it was more like coding non-player characters or computer opponents in a video game: programming independent, autonomous components in a system that could interact with one another and with their simulated environments. It was impossible not to anthropomorphize, impossible not to see the bits of code as little creatures, protohumans, let loose inside an infinite series of digital terrariums.

Eleanor and her colleagues gave the agents the ability to reproduce, to learn, to kill, to choose mates and wartime strategies, to be hostile or welcoming to outsiders, to be selfish or generous, honest or deceptive. They gave them goals and biases, conflicting and self-destructive desires, warped perceptions, genetic memory. They watched their empires rise and fall, watched them prosper and mutate through generations or wipe themselves out completely, then compared the results to the real world, to documented history and known, observable human behavior. The work straddled psychology, sociology, and computer science, and was infinitely more interesting to Eleanor than what they were doing in other labs in her department: artless, unromantic structural neuroscience—this goes here, that lights up there—or confederate-based studies on undergrads that were akin to pranks, tiny in focus and insignificant in participant numbers. Under Dr. Culver, it was trivial to run a simulation with a million agents, a million times. In the years she studied under him, funding for more and more powerful computers had rolled in.

She'd expected to be a researcher, not a clinician. She'd felt their lab was building to something revolutionary, a more general, fundamental understanding of human motivation, faster and more ethically than could be done using actual subjects. She was interested in people at the population level, in the universal, less so in filling her days with the texture and minutiae of their suffering, cooing as they cried in Teddy's white leather armchairs.

When Dr. Culver had first interviewed her, she'd ended up mentioning a familiar irony joked about among her classmates, perhaps among undergrad psychology students everywhere: It felt like the craziest among them were the ones continuing on to graduate and medical school.

Culver had understood it as a truism and not a joke. "Is it so surprising," he'd said, gravely, "that we would be interested in our own pathologies?"

There was a security camera in the hallway outside Dr. Culver's office. That camera became his savior and fixation in the eventual hearing, held in a seminar room in which she'd taught a class the semester before, the twenty-two-year-old graduate student ombudsman nervously taking notes at her side. "Yes, there was some mutual flirting that may have crossed a line," Dr. Culver said. His tone was impatient, almost droll, all of this beneath him, unworthy of his time. "But as the footage shows, my office door stayed open during the entire evening in question. If I had really assaulted her in the *graphic* manner she describes, wouldn't I have closed the door? Wouldn't I have been concerned about someone seeing or hearing this heinous crime I supposedly committed?"

She remembered staring at that door, from down on his faded oriental rug, and wondering the same thing.

In another meeting, the department chair noted—just an *observation*—that Eleanor was far enough in her combined master's-PhD coursework that she met the master's requirements. She could easily—and this was just a *suggestion*—rework her research into a master's thesis and graduate that spring. They would do everything they could to help get her out the door.

• • •

The previous summer, what she hadn't known would be her last summer of grad school, Eleanor had been casually dating a guy she'd met at a conference, another PhD student at a school in another state, four hours away. She answered ads on Craigslist and student listservs to find rides to visit him, getting into cars with random people off the internet, paying for gas in cash.

Once, a pair of brothers picked her up outside her lover's building at five in the morning. Their trunk was full of hand-painted tiles that they sold individually as art or in large batches to use as backsplashes and fireplace surrounds. The rear of their car sagged with the weight. In their limited but enthusiastic English, the two men told her they had a meeting in the city at nine with an important buyer, as explanation for why they were driving so thrillingly fast down the interstate, racing the dawn. They told jokes that made no sense in translation, and Eleanor laughed with them anyway. As they pulled up to her corner, having made the journey with time to spare, all three of them cheered.

The brothers refused her gas money and insisted on gifting her a tile. Two painted hummingbirds positioned head to tail, one orange and one blue, formed a yin-yang shape on the glazed ceramic square. To Eleanor, the birds represented the brothers, their kindness, the summer she had spent dozing trustingly against the car windows of total strangers as they always took her where they'd promised to go. The tile had vanished over the years, presumably broken or lost. She couldn't remember.

• • •

In the aftermath, at her mother's suggestion, Eleanor moved back into Lele's dark, cramped house. As she lay curled up on her childhood bed, less like a fetus than a fist, Lele stroked her hair, saying, "You just study. You help people like you always wanted. I'll take care of everything else." As she reworked her thesis, in the evenings, Lele pulled up a chair and sat beside her, silently keeping her on track. She would peel apples and pears with a knife, slice them inside her palm, and hand-feed segments to Eleanor. The first time, Eleanor hesitated, some part of her balking at her mother putting food directly into her adult mouth, but soon she could eat Lele's offerings without even taking her eyes off the screen. She appreciated that it kept her fingers and keyboard clean.

When Eleanor rubbed her straining eyes, Lele would say, "Go shower. Get ready for bed." And Eleanor would obey. One night, early on, Lele drew Eleanor's feet into her lap, over a piece of scrap paper, and clipped her toenails for her, which had grown into careless talons that pressed against the inside of her shoes. Eleanor listened to each discrete, percussive snap of the clippers, only dully aware of the pressure or pain of a bent nail. She felt a soothing, mindless distance from her own feet, from her whole body. She wished to abdicate her ownership of it, her responsibility for it, give it over to Lele's care.

Lele brought paperwork to Eleanor that Eleanor did not question, in the same manner Lele served her meals, putting a bowl of oatmeal or rice or a sheaf of documents on the table in front of her. "Eat this." "Sign here." "Your licensing exam is on the 27th."

Eventually, it was Lele who made her move out again, who found the apartment without Eleanor's involvement. She placed the rental agreement on the breakfast table with Eleanor's toast, already buttered and quartered. "It's time for you to go," she'd said, gently, and Eleanor obeyed. Later, she ran Eleanor's practice like a second full-time job, as secretary, accountant, assistant, more—she would do Eleanor's taxes, iron her blouses, shine her boots, maintain the illusion of their two separate homes. In addition to their Sunday visits, Lele regularly used her key to come by when Eleanor wasn't there, leaving cooked meals and groceries in the fridge, tidying in her wake, a benevolent, invisible force.

Eleanor sometimes thought of her first roommate, in her first off-campus apartment at the age of nineteen—a wide-eyed, freckle-faced girl named Ren. They'd met in the freshman dorms, after Eleanor started an electrical fire with a contraband space heater, and Ren started another a week later by boiling instant ramen inside a plug-in kettle. They'd correctly concluded they would annoy each other less than anyone else: Ren had grown up rich, and Eleanor had grown up with Lele. Ren came across as ditzy and oblivious, prone to locking herself out of her room and falling asleep with lit candles, while majoring in pure math on a dean's scholarship, and Eleanor had loved that, too, the seeming narrowness of her intelligence, her distracted genius.

She remembered how she and Ren had screamed and squealed when the dishwasher overflowed because Eleanor had loaded it with dish soap, when Ren lopped off the tip of her thumb with a cheap knife while trying to mince garlic, when they discovered what looked like a colony of mushrooms under the bath mat, when a plastic bowl melted in the microwave and filled the apartment with acrid, noxious fumes. Their high-pitched, girlish screeching, horror tinged with excitement, like they were only playing house, what had felt like ordinary growing pains. How lucky they had been, she thought, how privileged, to have this soft, low-stakes transition from teenage indolence to adulthood, to learn from only minor disasters.

She'd lost track of Ren in recent years. When she looked her up, Ren had a minimal, privated online presence, and Eleanor resisted the urge to dig deeper. She preferred to imagine Ren as wise and fully formed, looking back on their younger selves with laughter, her life golden and uninterrupted, marred by only one flattened thumb.

The last she'd heard, Dr. Culver's technology was now used mainly to plan the layouts of airports and retail stores, and was controversial even there—the agents being too rational, never rising to the variance and caprice of the human heart.

• • •

There was a low-budget TV show that played on the local station when Eleanor was a kid called *How Does the World Work?* Each episode consisted of two or three mini documentaries for children: a fireman in uniform explaining the parts of his truck, voice-over narration accompanying footage of packaged cookies being made on a factory line, an animated segment on the inner workings of a computer.

Eleanor hadn't especially liked this show, but whenever it came on, she watched the episode all the way through, just to hear the two versions of the theme song. The show opened with a montage of clips from past segments, interspersed with brief shots of kids posing against backgrounds of solid color, each making an exaggerated expression of wonderment or confusion. A trio of female voices—not in harmony, simply belting in unison—sang the theme, which had no lyrics other than *How does the world work?* The melody was high and repetitive, their voices breathy and strained over a stabbing synth, the emphasis on the line changing with repetition. The first two times, they sang it in a clunky rush: *How-does-the-world-work?* Then slower, landing hard on the last two words in turn: *How does the* WORLD *work? How does the world* WORK*?*

The closing credits played over a silent extension of whatever the last documentary segment had been—the firemen chatting amongst themselves in the firehouse garage, line workers gathered and waving in front of the factory, the animated guide through the computer dancing idly in place—while the invisible singers returned. This time, clustering the longer lyric to the same melody, they sang, *Now you know how the world works!*

Now YOU *know how the world works.*

Now you KNOW *how the world works.*

As a child, Eleanor could not stand to hear the opening version of the theme without hearing the closing one. There was something so satisfying about its resolution, a question answered.

The song would pop unexpectedly into her mind in adulthood, while she was walking on the street, or sitting in the department chair's office, or listening to her clients. The opener or the closer looping endlessly in her head, disconnected from its other half, without upbeat, simple explanations to link them. *How does the world work? How does the world work?*

Now you know how the world works. Now you know how the world works.

• • •

Lele would be aghast at her digital replacement, to see the prestige of Eleanor's career reduced to these underpaid, questionably legal video calls. Even dead, Lele felt more real, more present, than Eleanor's clients often did—their flat, pixelated, quarter-scale heads and truncated bodies, their scratchy voices that echoed off walls in faraway rooms.

When Eleanor had set up her profile on the online therapy platform initially, the app had helpfully told her which "tags" were experiencing the highest need, and she had ticked almost everything: *Anxiety*, *Depression*, *Life Coaching*, LGBTQ+ *Issues*,

Trauma, *Stress*, *Grief*, and *Sleep*, skipping only *Eating Disorders* and *Addiction*. She found these categorizations a little odd, a little too inclusive or exclusive, and she noted that all major personality, psychotic, and neurodevelopmental disorders were missing; she suspected the categories were decided by a Silicon Valley marketing team. These were the users they desired.

She had made an effort to keep up with the research, to read papers and listen halfheartedly to online conference presentations, but the platform had not asked for any proof she specialized or trained in these areas. There was no way to submit her degrees and licensure and postgraduate certificates for verification; she was allowed to input whatever title and suffixes she wanted in an open text field. Her license renewal was coming up, and she was toying with the idea of letting it expire, writing *life coach* or *counselor* without adjectives, or some other unprotected term. *Holistic healer. Professional listener.* When she had worked with Teddy, first under his supervision and then as a partner in their shared practice, she'd spent half her working hours keeping vigorous, methodical charts. The platform now automatically generated basic records, based on a couple of prompts at the end of each session, and she'd gotten increasingly lazy in her notes. She had left her time completely unblocked in the scheduling tab—nights, early mornings, weekends, holidays—and she sometimes went days without work, sometimes had clients back-to-back all day, and sometimes the platform created long, sleepless split shifts of unpaid time just too short to do anything else.

• • •

Almost as strange as seeing Lele again, resurrected in the daylight, was seeing her idle. Sitting unmoving at the dining table, her hands unoccupied, not running between a dozen tasks, solving another dozen problems in her head. When an alarming letter had arrived for Eleanor from the IRS, she didn't even read it all the way through before delivering it to Lele, who had smiled, bracingly, in the manner of an expert who relishes a challenge. Lele had cleaned the floors in Eleanor's apartment on her hands and knees, with a rag and a bucket of soapy water. When Eleanor suggested using a mop instead, she'd waved her away, saying, "It just doesn't get as clean that way."

Please say something, Eleanor thought.

What do you want me to say?

The voice didn't come from Lele but from behind Eleanor, above her—she turned in her seat, looking for the source. It was Lele's voice, if a little thinner, younger-sounding, tonally flatter. As she might sound through a laptop speaker. Or, she thought, a little more like Eleanor. Like Eleanor doing an impression of her mother. Their voices were not dissimilar.

When she turned back, the chair where Lele had sat was empty, tucked neatly back in place. She hadn't seen it move or heard it scrape the floor.

"Say something Mom would say," she whispered.

The voice came now from farther away. Whether from the entryway to her left or the kitchen to her right, she couldn't say. *What do you think I would say?*

Eleanor felt a sudden, crushing despair, heavy in her body, the gravity of a larger planet pulling her down. What would Lele say? What would Lele do? She asked herself these questions all the time, her answers feeble and uncertain, never knowing if she was right. She'd made this ghost. It couldn't tell her anything new.

6

The downpour continued all day. Eleanor began unpacking her suitcase and boxes, but she hated the look of her shoddy things in the new house, which had seemed perfect before she arrived. The entryway had no closet, nowhere to store anything. She pulled her raincoat from a box and left the rest of her ratty jackets and shoes inside.

When she lifted her head, Lele stood in the far corner, her back pressed against the wall. Her expression was watchful, her presence strangely inert, as though to say, silently, *Don't mind me.*

Already Eleanor felt inured to this vision, resigned to her mind's persistent conjuring. Lele off to the side, always there, appearing suddenly in rooms as she had in Eleanor's thoughts. Was it so different, she thought, from how she'd already been living?

She set up her coffee machine in the kitchen. Half the multicolored cabinets had open shelves, and they were made yet more chaotic by her cracked and mismatched dishes.

In the late afternoon, she decided to drive back into Bering Rock for groceries. As she locked the door, the key stuck again, needing to be wriggled and then wrenched out.

Standing by her car, she looked back at the house, uneasy again at how clearly one could see inside. She thought of the tension curtain rod she had in her bedroom window in the old apartment, the nap of the cheap fabric. She had not thought to bring it, but it wouldn't fit the dimensions of these enormous windows anyway. There came a sound from the woods that sounded to Eleanor like a hooting owl, though it was still light out.

The swing gate was closed when she reached it. She pulled her hood over her head. The car idling, in the glare of her headlights, she pushed the gate to the side, the wet metal bar stingingly cold in her hands. She was sure she'd left it open the day before. The car played a patient *ding ding ding* of warning: keys in the ignition, lights on, door ajar, seat belt unbuckled.

The grocery store was a stand-alone building clad in corrugated metal sheeting like a barn. Eleanor dashed through the rain from her parking spot, the lot empty aside from an RV with windows blacked out by cardboard. The hood of her jacket was slightly too small, and the hair at the front of her face dripped rainwater into her collar.

Inside, fluorescent panels hung from the exposed roof on long, ropy wires, so low a taller customer could reach up and touch them. It was expansive inside, with a dozen checkout lanes, but as far as Eleanor could see, there was only one person working, a single cashier checking out a single customer, who walked out as Eleanor walked in. The butcher, deli, and bakery counters were all dark, the lights off in the spaces behind, the display coolers covered by tarps. Classic rock played from an unseen source so softly she could have been imagining it, the high notes of a yearning saxophone sometimes breaking into her awareness.

She didn't see any other customers as she proceeded through the store. At first, she thought she saw more employees—restocking produce, setting up price reduction tags in the canned goods, emerging from a back room with a mop—but soon realized it was the same cashier she'd seen when she came in, over and over, as though she would complete a task and teleport to another section whenever Eleanor looked away.

When Eleanor went to check out, the cashier was already waiting back at her till. She looked down as she scanned each item, so Eleanor was free to stare at her, a three-dimensional person in real space. She was tall and broad, with a plump, ageless face that radiated competence—the kind of face that had likely followed her from childhood and was easy to imagine in old age.

"Where are you headed in this terrible weather?" she asked.

"Nowhere. Home," Eleanor said. Home, she repeated to herself, marveling at the thought.

"Ah. Back to the city? Hike get washed out?"

"No, I live here. I just moved here."

The cashier looked up, still holding an apple aloft. "Here, here? As in Bering Rock?"

"Yes. Well, sort of. The new development up the road."

The cashier mouthed *new development*, as though trying to remember the meaning of words in a foreign language. "Oh! In the valley? Off the mountain road? I think I heard that a new developer bought the land, but I didn't realize construction had started again. Let alone that it was ready for people to move in."

"It didn't. Construction will resume next year."

"Then where are you living?"

"In one of the houses that was already finished."

Eleanor felt conscious of the apple still in the woman's hand, which she was suddenly gripping too hard, bruising the flesh under her thumb. "In . . ." she repeated, trailing off. To Eleanor's relief, she put down the apple on the belt. "Which one?"

She'd spoken so quietly Eleanor wasn't sure that she'd heard correctly. "Pardon?"

"Which house? The model home or the other one?"

"I thought they were both model homes. Mine is the one with the white window frames."

The tension in the cashier's brow eased slightly, suggesting Eleanor had chosen the better of bad options.

"Do you know if anyone is living in the other house?" Eleanor asked.

This woman had a wonderfully expressive face, Eleanor thought, watching it twist, her thoughts open to the world. "I can't believe nobody told you," she said.

Eleanor thought of the many documents she hadn't read before submitting her offer, including nineteen pages subheaded *Disclosures*.

"The original developer went bankrupt—"

"I know about that," Eleanor interjected, relieved.

"It was a big deal around here. Basically everyone I know worked on that site, clearing the land, laying the lines. They worked incredibly fast. The forest was there, and then it was gone. I drove my boyfriend to work one morning, and when you looked down on the valley, it was like watching ants swarming on a hill—there were that many men."

She pictured this quantity of men with machines for stripping and felling and gathering logs as more like locusts than ants, a sweeping pestilence devouring its way across the valley, leaving nothing behind.

"This guy was some real estate millionaire who showed up out of nowhere. When people talked about him at the bar, we used the phrase 'richer than god.' And then suddenly he wasn't. Suddenly there were days the land sat empty, or people walked off in the middle of a job, leaving their work exposed to the elements. Rented equipment went walking. Nobody could believe it, at first. When he stopped paying his invoices, his subcontractors, it felt like the whole town collapsed.

"They were supposed to lay all the foundations at once, do all the plumbing and framing at the same time, but instead the reduced crews focused on completely finishing just two. Two houses, all the way to the fixtures, the floors, the paint. One model home so future owners could be convinced to invest now, keep the project alive, and one for him. *For him*," the cashier repeated. "Our millionaire was going to live on-site, in one of those little houses on an unpaved road, through months or years of noise and mess. That's when we should have known."

None of this information was surprising to Eleanor. She could have guessed it all, from what she'd seen, the few facts she'd had. The feeble beginnings of homes in the valley, the capped piping and temporary arrangements of plywood, piles of loose brick, everything washed away, blown over, cracked in the sun. What struck her instead was the way the cashier spoke in the first-person plural, so definitively part of a *we*, speaking for a whole town. Eleanor remembered when she had felt that way, in her family of two, any internal discord—thin towels, bad coffee—trifling beside the surety of their shared goals and beliefs. *We*, always, meaning Eleanor and Lele. How much easier it had been to want whatever Lele wanted, to do whatever she said. How safe it had made her feel.

"I'm sorry," Eleanor said, for lack of anything else to say.

The cashier waved this away. Pity was not the point of her story. "Once he was completely out of money, when he owed—I don't know, probably hundreds of thousands of dollars, maybe millions, he holed up in the house they'd built. He didn't answer the door to any of his debtors, or suits from the banks. Sometimes former workmen would get drunk and go over in packs, saying they'd break down the door and rough him up. As far as I know, nobody did more than ring his bell and shout threats.

"He didn't come out for weeks, didn't come into town for food or anything else. Not that we would have served him. I assumed at some point that he'd left, just driven away in the night without anyone knowing.

"So one night, another group of guys start talking big at the bar, and then they drive, hammered, to the old site, to try and have it out with him again. They get there, and there's a light on in his house, upstairs, and a light on in the trailer on the hill—the site office. The office door is unlocked, so they check inside, but he's not there. They go back to his house, even more riled up now. They ring the bell, pound on the door, peer in the windows. They stand on the front lawn and holler for him to come out. And then—*bang*!"

The cashier slammed her hand, palm down, onto the belt. The sharp sound rang out in the store, silent but for the murmuring music, the hum of the lights and the refrigerator condensers, silent of any other human movement or speech. She waited, head tilted, for Eleanor to react.

"He shot himself," Eleanor said. Her throat caught on the beginning of the sentence, the *he* a hoarse noise, only *shot himself* articulated cleanly.

The cashier made a gun of her hand, pressing the muzzle of her index and middle fingers upward beneath her chin. "Right here," she said.

"When did this happen?"

Her gaze and hands abruptly dropped. She resumed scanning Eleanor's purchases. She looked dazed, emotion draining from her face—an unseemly, frenzied glee, clear only in its passing. She liked telling this story; she was good at it. She liked the ending. "March."

"*March*? Of this year?" Something about the mythic, well-worn nature of the telling had made Eleanor imagine the events in a distant past. Even though she could picture, in a slow-dawning part of her mind, the year of construction of her home, printed in the original listing and the parts of the documents that she hadn't ignored. It was this year.

"Mmm-hmm."

At a loss again, Eleanor said, "That's so sad."

The cashier looked up sharply. "Sad," she repeated. The word sounded absurd and inadequate. "For who?"

She had been trying to help Eleanor, to warn her. But in Eleanor's sympathy for a man hounded to suicide by an angry mob, she had apparently misunderstood, missed something important. Sided against the cashier, against Bering Rock. "For everyone," Eleanor said, lamely.

The cashier snorted. She dumped Eleanor's purchases in a bag, scooping them at random with both hands, loose apples on the bottom. "That'll be $68.55."

• • •

Eleanor drove carefully, the rain coating the windshield in rippling waves, the wipers squeaking in a frantic rhythm. The spring and summer had been spent in a statewide drought, the reservoirs still low despite the wet weather of the last few weeks. She found herself thinking of Antoni again. She'd felt ambivalent about the bodies of many of the men she'd slept with in her life, but she had truly loved his: his strong arms and soft belly, every inch of him covered in whorls of dark hair.

He had asked her once, gently, as though leading her by the hand toward a vista he wished her to see, what she would do when her mother died. She'd never pictured it. She understood outliving one's parents was the natural order of things, but deep down she had always expected to die young while Lele lived past a hundred, past two hundred, became the oldest woman ever to walk the earth. Eleanor saw herself as uncommonly fragile, physically, and Lele as uncommonly hardy. With their flesh stripped away, she imagined Lele's skeleton made of steel, and hers of the chalky sugar in candy hearts, something that dissolved in the mouth and crumbled when pressed.

To Antoni, she'd blurted out, "I'd kill myself."

She had immediately regretted saying this. She regretted it more now, knowing that it had not turned out to be true.

The swing gate was open and waiting, a long neon streak on the side of the road. She could see only a narrow, intermittent gap between curtains of rain and nearly missed the turn. She carefully rode the brake down the steep hill.

The cruelest thing Antoni had ever said, at the end of their relationship: "I used to feel sorry for you. I thought she was smothering you, stunting you. But now I feel sorry for *her*. She's a fucking saint."

When the houses appeared, the endlessly burning light in the construction office, Eleanor heard the cashier's voice, her hand smacking the conveyor belt. *Bang!* She could see it all, blurred by the rain: the shouting men on the lawn, leering in the windows, demanding he come out and face them. How they jumped as one, immediately sobered, when they heard the shot.

7

Eleanor ran from the car to the door. When she put her key in the lock, it hit resistance about a third of the way in. She shimmied it in and out, feeling for the grooves without success. She braced against the frame and pushed harder.

She felt it lodge inside.

The key would not turn. She couldn't remove it either, her fingers slipping off the thin clover of wet brass.

Her jacket was saturated, the nylon deflating and clinging to her body. She ran back to the car. She called the first result for *locksmith in my area*, which promised twenty-minute arrival times. A dispatcher brusquely told her she was outside their range. She tried five more numbers. The fourth said he could come out to Bering Rock, but when she gave her location in more detail, he interrupted: "Sorry, no private roads. Company policy." The final locksmith said he could come in the morning. She was about to agree—she could drive back to the apartment for the night—when he added, "Or I can give you the number of a buddy of mine. He can probably get out there right now. If you can't get a hold of him, call me back."

She felt unaccountably moved, parched for basic kindness. She put the phone on speaker so she could take down the number in her notes app.

The person on the other end answered with, "Yeah?"

Practiced now, she quickly explained how she got his number and her situation, that she lived in a new development on an unnamed road off the mountain road out the back of Bering Rock. *There's a frog on the bump on the log in the hole in the bottom of the sea*, she thought, wearily. "Do you know it?"

"Yeah, I know it. I can help you out." He had a sluggish way of speaking, drawing out the ends of words and the spaces between. "Are you alone?"

Out of the corner of her eye, she saw Lele in the passenger seat. She looked somehow denser, more solid, than she had that morning or the night before—like what Eleanor had seen before had been an empty, flaccid sack, since filled with grain. Or a line drawing, now flooded with watercolor paint. Lele shook her head vigorously, her lips pursed. This time, over her deathbed pajamas, she wore her quilted winter coat unzipped, as though she'd had to rush out on an errand in the middle of the night.

After Eleanor had moved out the first time, at eighteen, Lele had pretended to all tradespeople who came to the house that she was married, going so far as to wear a cheap ring and put out a pair of size-eleven men's boots bought at the thrift store. "So they don't come back to rob an old lady living alone," she'd explained. In her youth, Eleanor had found this habit amusingly paranoid, had suppressed a smile when Lele added a pair of equally large house moccasins—"Even men own more than one pair of shoes," she'd said, humorlessly—and only later did it strike her as sad, this imaginary protector and his unfilled, foot-shaped hollows. And only now, considering the locksmith's question, what his motivation could possibly be for asking if she was alone, did Eleanor wonder if Lele had been only prudent, if she'd been right all along.

Tell him you're waiting for your husband, Lele said. That's what Lele would have said.

But the lie would be obvious when he arrived, Eleanor thought. Somehow. She had no shoes to put out. And Lele wasn't here, not really. "Yes," she said.

"Mmm-kay. Give me, like, an hour."

After two hours, Eleanor called the number again, and didn't get an answer. She was shivering in her drenched clothes. The heater in the old car took forever to get going, so when she turned on the engine, the vents blew cold air into her face, and she was afraid she'd kill the battery if she waited for it to warm.

She considered leaving a message telling him to forget it, and then calling the locksmith who'd recommended him and asking him to meet her in the morning. But Lele shook her head again, painting a wordless image of the *yeah?* locksmith arriving after a long drive in the rain, to an empty house with a stuck key and no payment, no witnesses around for miles. Letting himself in, helping himself to her laptop, trashing the place out of spite.

The transition to night had been subtle—the daytime sky dim and blackened with clouds, the relentless rain blanketing the car windows, warping and distancing the world outside—but now it was absolute.

Her phone finally rang after nearly three hours. "Hey," he said, without preamble or apology, "I've been driving back and forth on the mountain road, but I can't seem to find the turn-off. Do you have a car? Could you drive up to the top and wait with your lights on? Or if you don't, stand there with a flashlight or something?"

"Are you past the swing gate?"

"Yeah. I think so."

He thinks so? Lele said. *What the hell does that mean?*

Eleanor did as he asked: She drove back up the hill, pulled to the side as best she could at the intersection with the mountain road, her right tires tipping into the ditch, and parked. Her headlights projected small, murky puddles of light, barely penetrating the downpour, the pitch-black night.

Lele's seat belt was buckled too tight across the chest, the strap digging into the diamond-shaped padding of her coat. *If the battery dies now, you'll really be in trouble*, she said.

"I know," Eleanor said, aloud.

After another twenty minutes, she finally saw headlights, approaching surprisingly fast from the direction she was facing. She leaned on her horn to get his attention.

He pulled up alongside her car and rolled down his window. Their cars were almost touching, the road not quite wide enough for two. She rolled down her window and rain immediately blew inside. He was shouting something, but she couldn't hear him over the wind, a wall of water between them.

"What?" she shouted back.

"You lead!" he bellowed.

She gingerly navigated her car around his, hoping he could discern the shape of the tight turn as they crept back to her house in the dark. She glanced into her rearview mirror periodically but could make out only a silhouette in the driver's seat.

After she pulled to a stop, he parked so close behind, their bumpers just kissed. The wind was less intense down in the valley, but as their headlights extinguished at the same time, as her engine went silent, the night seemed to howl.

She got out of her car first, her useless jacket immediately flattened again. As her eyes adjusted, she got her first clear look at the car and the man exiting it. The ancient, champagne-colored sedan had a crumpled dent to the passenger door—the imprint of another car's nose, the hood pinched upward on the same side. The locksmith was tall and rangy, a bag of tools with a long strap hanging from his shoulder. She gestured toward the house, and as she got closer, walking alongside him, she realized he might be the tallest person she'd ever seen. Taller than the doorframe, his arms too long for his denim jacket, his thin wrists and knuckles exposed.

He dismantled the entire lockset of the door with alarming speed, holding a flashlight in his mouth. She hovered behind, dripping like she had just emerged from the sea.

Two empty holes were left in the door. He hooked his fingers into the lower hole and swung the door toward himself, then stepped inside. She hurried in afterward and turned on the lights.

He did not look as drenched as she felt, water pooling around her shoes, cascading from her shoulders and hair. Perhaps in his early forties, his face weather-beaten, hollow-cheeked, raw around the nose. He squinted against the light.

He held out his hand to shake hers, his nails black with grease. Both his hand and hers were cold and damp, death clasping death. She clenched her whole body, trying not to shiver, overwhelmed by the relief of the warm house. A chill had settled deep within her while she waited for hours in the car.

"I'm Richie," he said.

The name didn't suit him, a boy's name on this ragged, starved-looking giant, leaning so far in her direction it seemed like he would tip over.

"Eleanor."

She felt him looking her up and down, her clothes plastered to her body. The tip of his pink tongue flashed, wetting his lips.

"Can you . . . fix the lock?" she said. "Put the handle back?"

"Of course," he said, his words as slow and stretched as they had been on the phone, as though they took a long time to travel from his mind to his lungs to his mouth.

"I'm going to go change."

He smiled at that, the corner of his distant mouth lifting as he bent toward her like a drooping flower. She winced. "I'll bring you a towel," she added.

She looked back as she climbed the stairs. He hadn't moved except to stand up straight, continuing to smile at her. Half-way up the flight of stairs, she thought his head still seemed higher than hers.

She closed the bedroom door. She heard Lele, muffled, as though she stood on the other side: *Put a chair under the doorknob.* But there was no chair in the bedroom, just the beautiful wooden bed and the beautiful wooden nightstands and half-unpacked boxes that weren't the right dimensions to wedge the knob.

The towel under the window was wetter than it had been when she'd left it that morning. She lifted it, and it was sopping, saturated through, dripping from the corners. She threw it down again. A problem for later. She threw her jacket on top, wet heap on wet heap.

She rooted through a box of clothes, unearthed a sweatshirt, sweatpants, underwear, and socks, and changed as fast as she could directly behind the door, holding it shut, drying her skin with any incompletely soaked spot of the clothes she'd been wearing. Her skin was freezing to the touch. Her teeth chattered, a tremble quaking through her. She found another sweatshirt and a second pair of socks to layer on top. She hadn't thought to take a towel from the box on the landing on her way. She squeezed out her hair over the sodden towel and jacket on the floor.

When she came down, carrying a towel for Richie, she saw he'd spread a puffy gray blanket on the entryway floor, stained with streaks of what she hoped were grease and rust, black and copper red. He'd laid out the parts of the door handle and dead bolt on top, down to the screws, the opposing faceplate, and, already freed, the key. He was spraying each one with an aerosol can, wiping them off with a rag. They looked small and toylike in his hands, exposed as the security theater they were.

He didn't thank her as he took the towel, just rubbed it against his face, over his shorn head, his hair buzzed close to the skull. "The keyhole filled with gunk from the rain," he said. He gestured at the two holes, the door punctuated with a colon, where cold air and a mist of rain were getting in. "The rain picks up dirt and debris, runs into the holes, and gums up the pins. It's going to keep happening. It'll only get worse once it starts rusting, or when the water freezes over the winter—you don't have an awning or anything over the door. The water just runs straight down the front of your house, straight over the lock."

She remembered finding the flat, featureless front of the house elegant and modern. "You can't get a door lock wet?"

"You can't pour water into it all day long." Richie pushed open the door, which swung with a disturbing weightlessness under the force of one hand. "You should have something like that."

She walked to the threshold. It took her a moment to understand he was pointing at the house across the street, and longer still to see what he meant, peering through the rain—easing slightly now—and the darkness. Across her front yard, across the road, across the yard facing opposite. The structure of the other house had a subtly different shape, the second floor jutting out over the first by a few feet, above the front door.

She was still staring out the door when he said, "You know what happened there?"

Eleanor could feel him standing behind her, leaning over her shoulder—over her head. "Someone told me just today," she replied.

"Can't say I feel all that sorry for the bastard."

She felt the heat of Richie at her back and recoiled from it, even as she still felt cold. The chill from the outside air and a chill from within, like a shard of ice in her gut. She saw the cashier's face, her eyes bright with excitement, mouth twisted, resisting a smile. Pitiless. "Nobody does," she murmured.

"When I was a kid, this valley was all trees. Hell, it was trees just a couple years ago. There was only a little clearing, from an old fire, filled with wildflowers." He pointed into the night. "That hillside used to be so steep, it was like a wall. I couldn't believe it when they built a road that could handle those big trucks and machines." Richie was quiet for a moment, as though reminiscing. "Why is the office light on?" he asked. "Is someone in there? Have they started work again?"

"I don't know. It's always on. I've never seen it off." She turned. He was so close to her, bent so low, that their faces were only inches apart. She stumbled back, her sock foot catching on the lip of the door and landing outside, wet again. He reached as though to catch her with his freakishly long arms. The door handle he was cleaning still hung off the long, bony pinky of his left hand. He could support its weight with his smallest finger.

She dodged around him, suddenly furious. "Can you hurry this up? You said you'd be here in an hour, and I was waiting for you in the cold for over three." She was shivering again, which only made her angrier.

He blinked slowly. "Not many people would come in this weather," he said, each word an eternity. "All the way out here, in the dark. Not going to be an easy drive back, either."

"It wasn't dark when I called," she snapped. She didn't want him to know he was right, that no one else had been willing to come. That no one would come.

"I just have a soft heart, see. I couldn't leave a young lady trapped *all by herself*, without a soul around to help."

Eleanor had a theory that she had never shared with anyone, not even Lele, that this happened to her so much not because she was attractive but because she was plain. That her plainness was what made men feel entitled to her.

"I'll leave you to it, then," she said.

She clutched her elbows as she moved through the living room to the kitchen, resisting the urge to run. She waited to see if he would follow her. When he did not, when the soft clink of metal suggested he had resumed cleaning and reinstalling the lock, she resumed breathing.

She badly wanted a hot drink, to feel warmed on the inside. Her groceries were still in the car, but she had a half bag of ground coffee she'd brought from the apartment.

The coffeemaker burbled, dispensed, clicked. She pulled the pot from the hot plate, poured a mug, replaced the pot, and when she turned back around, Richie was standing with her in the kitchen. She gasped but maintained her grip on the mug.

Richie was smiling, as though their last conversation hadn't happened. "All done," he said, singsong. He inhaled theatrically, his nostrils flaring. "That coffee sure smells good."

She put down her mug. She stepped past him, walking in long, swift strides to the entryway. The lock and handle were back in place.

"Good as new," he said, appearing again behind her. He moved quickly and noiselessly for someone so large. He held the door open and slid in the key, demonstrated the dead bolt turning smoothly back and forth. "But like I said, you need to get someone to install some kind of awning over the door, or this is going to just keep happening. Also—did you notice there's water coming in through your windows?"

Her mouth fell open. She felt sick at the realization he'd been in her bedroom.

Richie pointed to the base of the floor-to-ceiling windows on either side of the front door. There was a thin line of darkened concrete flooring before each one.

"Might just be the weather stripping or the caulking. I can recommend a guy—"

"It's fine, I'll get it fixed." She felt a desperate, overriding desire to get Richie out of her house. Everything else—a new, separate leak—paled in comparison. "May I have my key back?"

He held out her house key, which looked like it belonged to a locket or a child's diary between his fingers. She reached for it, and he snatched it back playfully.

Stone-faced, she said, "Give me my key."

His smile finally dropped. He let her take the key, but then wrapped his hand around hers, encasing her hand and the key entirely within his fist.

She tried to pull away, but his grip was strong, immobile. She had to make this end. "Thank you," she said, her voice high. "What do I owe you?"

From the hunched posture he used to talk to her, down at her eye level, he stretched to his full height, distant as a god. He held her in place by the fist, his eyes slightly unfocused, as though counting off the seconds.

Nearly a minute went by before he let her yank her hand free. Everything she did, it was because he allowed it.

"Six hundred," he said.

The first place she'd called, the one with the twenty-minute promise and the dispatcher, had advertised a seventy-five-dollar rate for residential lockouts. "Are you serious?"

He stared at her for a long moment. "Emergency fee," he began, lingering over each syllable. "Inclement weather fee. Outside of business hours fee. Extended mileage fee. Oh wait, I forgot the being a bitch who couldn't give me a fucking cup of coffee and talk like a human being fee. *Eight* hundred."

Lele stood on the stairs. She leaned over the railing, outraged. *Don't pay him a dime! Call the cops!*

But Lele wasn't here. Eleanor imagined Richie talking to a cop on her front lawn, if one ever came. What exactly had he done wrong? *I performed the requested service, officer, and now she's refusing to pay.* Eight hundred dollars to make him go away. The number was meaningless—whatever it took to make it go away. "Is a check okay?" she said.

"Sure," he said. "And I know you won't do anything dumb, like try to cancel it or let it bounce." He didn't have to say why. That he knew where she lived, alone in this wasteland, and now they both understood locks to be a fiction.

8

Eleanor stayed up the rest of the night. She took a long, hot shower, still struggling to get warm. She bundled herself again in several layers. She flipped her head upside down to dry her hair with a towel. When she stood up straight, she saw Lele in the mirror, at the edge of the reflection—Lele was standing on the opposite side of the bathroom, wedged in the corner. She was still wearing her coat, looking around, admiring the tiled walls. *This room would be good in an earthquake*, she said, in her Eleanor-puppet voice. *Or a drive-by shooting. No windows.*

"A drive-by shooting," Eleanor repeated.

You never know.

Were these things Lele actually would have said? Her overpreparation and paranoia that had been mostly useful, only lightly absurd, her mind like the overstuffed purse of the idealized mother, containing everything anyone could ever need. But no—she'd been more knowing and complicated than Eleanor could invent.

Eleanor duct-taped a garbage bag over the door lock to keep the rain out. She tried opening and closing the leaking bedroom window over and over, until it felt—maybe—like the sash sat more firmly in place, like the locks were catching properly. So much rain had blown in during her attempts that it was hard to tell if it was still leaking. She put a fresh towel on the floor, squeezed out the old one and hung it up to dry with her raincoat in the bathroom. Lele followed her around the house, always appearing on the other side of the room, in the farthest corner from Eleanor.

Eleanor only remembered her groceries around one a.m. Lele ventured closer, sitting at the island counter as Eleanor unloaded the bags, the ice cream now a softly frozen core in a tub of soup. One of the drawer pulls, a metal bar extending past its two prongs—each drawer having a different style of handle—caught at her sweater each time she passed, the knit snagged just above her hip. She'd bought what she'd thought of as essentials in the moment: fruit, white bread, peanut butter, instant noodles, hot dogs, eggs, coffee.

You didn't buy any vegetables? Or meat? Or rice?

Lined up on the counter, her choices felt meager and embarrassing, the shopping list of a child going camping. The apartment fridge was full of expired sauces that Lele thought she would use to cook when she moved in, not knowing how quickly she would be bedridden, laid flat. Eleanor had thrown away the twenty-pound bag of rice Lele had bought, crawling with weevils after her death. Eleanor often stretched one take-out meal over three days.

She wanted to turn on all the lights, flush the darkness from every corner, but she lived in an illuminated fishbowl, vulnerable from all sides. She browsed custom curtains online, estimating the size and number of her windows to put together an order on a couple of websites, but she must have been doing something wrong, because the totals were astronomical. A single panel came up as $400. Her apartment had come with blinds in the main room, and she'd bought the bedroom curtain for $13, including the rod. She texted Matt. *Do you know where I can get some blinds/curtains big enough for these windows?* After a moment, she added, *Also can you recommend someone who can fix leaky windows and install an awning?*

She shouldn't have been surprised that he answered immediately, at two thirty a.m. *Yes! I have recommendations for both. Sharing contacts now.*

At three a.m., she told herself she could still sleep for a couple of hours, if she went to bed now. She thought the same thing at four and then five. She worked her way through the pot of coffee.

• • •

She had a session at seven a.m., a new client named David. At the old building, with Teddy, she'd had an elaborate intake process, a therapeutic plan template she'd adapted from examples in her postgrad training. She didn't bother with that anymore, now that more than half her sessions were first sessions. She asked basic questions that were already in their profiles—age, job, marital status—and then, simply, "What brings you to therapy?"

David was drawn, nebbishy-looking, sitting far back from his webcam. Round glasses perched on his nose. The unsteady neck of a turtle above a graphic T-shirt. "My wife thought it would be a good idea," he said. "She thinks I get too worked up about the news. She says I'm too negative, and I talk about depressing stuff all the time, and it's making people not want to be around me. Including her."

"I see. Do you agree with that assessment?"

"Maybe. I don't know. We had a big fight recently. She said I care more about strangers than about her."

"What made her feel that way?"

"No one thing, I don't think. Just like—sometimes she'll ask me, you know, what color of throw pillow I like better. And it's like, the world is going to end in six years. People are dying. Who cares about a fucking throw pillow? Sorry."

"No need to apologize. You can swear."

David blinked rapidly. The permission to swear seemed to register as some other kind of permission, and he spoke as though unleashing the words, as though he'd tried and failed to hold them back. "I feel like every day, there's some new horror. Some new, specific detail, proof of the planet dying even faster than we thought. Something irrevocably lost, some way that things will be worse forever from now on. I feel like the entire country, the entire world, is constantly in the middle of another natural disaster. Every week there's a once-in-a-century event somewhere. Except here."

"Here?" Eleanor repeated.

"*Right* here," he clarified. "Like, right where I'm standing, like I'm the luckiest motherfucker in the universe. Like we live in some kind of oasis, some eye of the storm. All this violence and death swirling around us while we debate throw pillows. My wife wanted to talk about contributing more to our retirement accounts, maybe retiring early, and I wanted to laugh. We're not going to retire! The earth is going to be uninhabitable long before that."

"Have you only started to feel this way recently? Does your wife describe this as a change in your behavior?"

"No, not at all. When we were first dating, she used to tease me about it. She called me Eeyore. Like, the depressed donkey. I guess it didn't use to bother her so much." David adjusted his glasses. "Sometimes I look over at her phone, and her feed is full of her friends' pictures, and strangers living these aspirational fantasies. Some random lady in a white dress with a white couch and a white kitchen, baking a chocolate cake with her toddler without getting chocolate on anything."

Eleanor looked past her screen to the room around her. The pale furniture still unmarred, the museum quality of the concrete and wood, the tall, naked sheets of glass.

"And it feels almost unfair that my feed is so different, and she gets to be so oblivious, so heartless. Every morning, I wake up and see children being slaughtered. Dictators getting elected, rights stripped away, workers mistreated, missiles fired. In a sick way, I almost miss the early days of the pandemic. I miss *lockdown*. Because then there was an explanation for why I was so slow at work, why I was upset all the time. A reason that everyone understood. For a brief moment, the whole world acknowledged that everything is terrible and fucked and broken—we were finally in agreement about that. Everyone finally agreed with me. I think—I think that time was the most hopeful I'd ever been. It felt like we'd hit some kind of rock bottom, where everything was plastic and big, systemic changes might be possible. And then nothing happened. Everything went back to the way it was, or worse."

In one of her first programming classes, within the psychology department, Eleanor remembered learning about the DOCTOR variation of the 1960s chatbot ELIZA, which used a remarkably small amount of code to mimic a Rogerian, person-centered therapist. ELIZA-DOCTOR repeated inputs in the form of questions, and said things like "I see" and "What do you think?" and "Please go on" when stumped. "An active listener," their professor had said dryly. "She lets you reach your own conclusions without judgment." ELIZA was no sophisticated AI—the script was easy to understand, easy to improve, and Eleanor and her classmates had done so for fun, incorporating new rules and reassembled sentence formats, making her sound more natural, more up-to-date, more human. Talking to her was maddening, funny, a little insulting, to the profession they were pursuing, to the science they believed in.

"Please go on," Eleanor said.

About forty minutes into their fifty-minute session, Eleanor decided she needed to give David something actionable or he might not come back. "Have you heard of having a 'worry time'?"

"No."

"I'll send you a worksheet. But the basic idea is that you choose a time, each day, dedicated to worrying. And throughout the day, as anxious thoughts occur to you, you put them off until worry time. You say to yourself, 'I'll think about that at three o'clock,' and try to focus on the task in front of you. On, for example, being less slow at work. Being present with your wife and listening to her concerns, even frivolous ones."

The quality of the video call was better than it had been the past two days. Perhaps the load on the cell towers was lower this early in the morning. She could read David's skepticism, his head cocked, chin turned slightly away from the camera. No, more than skepticism. Revulsion. She pressed on anyway. "And when worry time rolls around, you spend a set amount of time—twenty minutes, let's say—writing out everything that's troubling you, all your fears and concerns. You can also spend that time brainstorming solutions."

"Solutions," he repeated. "I'm going to come up with solutions in twenty minutes a day. To what? Climate change? Genocide? Capitalism?"

"You could also spend that time actively engaged in the causes you care about. Let's say, every day at three, you donate a small amount of money, whatever you can afford. Or you write or call your representatives, or you research volunteer opportunities and protests in your area. So every day, you've done something positive and concrete." She could tell David was rallying, gearing up to argue. "Or that's the only time you read the news. You stay up-to-date by reading it once a day, but it doesn't consume your whole day. It doesn't set the tone for the day the second you're awake." Despite herself, Eleanor imagined programming this speech into ELIZA.

He stared straight into the camera now, his jaw tight. "You talk," he began, slowly, "as though the people in the news live in a different dimension. Or like they're animals at the zoo. I can look in on them, feel bad, throw some pittance their way, and then look away the rest of the time, go back to my dimension where everything is sunshine and rainbows. Like none of this affects me. Like none of this is my fault."

"Does your distress help them, materially? Or does it just hurt you, hurt your wife? Does it, in fact, make you less able to help others, less able to do good work in the world, because you're so paralyzed by all this anger and pain?"

David didn't answer immediately. She read resentment and defeat in his expression—she'd had a rational victory, not an emotional one, and those never took.

"I'm not angry," he said, finally. "I know I seem angry, and my wife thinks I'm angry all the time. And I'm not trying to be a sanctimonious jerk, when I ask her, you know, who made the throw pillow, how were they treated, how was it packaged, how was it shipped. And I'm not being . . . altruistic, not really. When she shows me the pillow, I feel—I feel afraid."

A pop-up in the corner reminded Eleanor they were almost out of time. Her instinct was to praise him for this admission, to pat them both on the back for arriving here so quickly, to tell him how much she looked forward to unpacking it next time.

Out the window, behind her computer, the rain was easing with daybreak, the overcast sky silvery to the east, but the wind was only getting worse. She could see the upper branches of the bordering trees swaying in unison. She imagined the locksmith among them, watching her, even taller than he had been. His head as high as the treetops, moving with the branches in their ritual dance.

"Do you know what you're afraid of?" she said.

"Earthquakes. The stock market crashing. The guillotine." He smiled wanly. "But not really. It's more like, we live in a fantasy. Me and my wife. A dream. A sandcastle as the tide is coming in. And one day we'll wake up in the gutter where everyone else lives, where we belong, and all this *stuff*, the home decor and the retirement accounts, will be worthless. Will turn out to have been more sand, more dreams."

The pop-up began blinking angrily. "Our time is up," she said.

9

Eleanor's next appointment was at four p.m. She'd been sitting rigidly on the unyielding wood of the dining chair, made by the man who'd killed himself across the street. Her body ached. She took another shower, still feeling that damp cold that seemed to originate inside her, like a wet rag wrapped around her spine. She turned the water to scalding as it beat down upon the back of her stiff neck.

Too wired to try sleeping, she decided to go back to the apartment for more of her things. The sky was an abrupt, blazing, amnesiac blue, like the rain had never happened. The trees creaked as they rubbed against one another in the wind, fallen deadwood pinned between living trunks, the sound sometimes like a swinging screen door, sometimes like a squealing, chittering bird. As she drove up the hill, she noticed that most of the other homesites had filled with half a foot of standing water.

The gate was closed. She couldn't imagine Richie getting out of his mangled car to close it behind him the night before. The leaves of the underbrush flickered and waved like miniature flags from either side of the road.

There was no one on the streets in Bering Rock. The grocery store parking lot, as she passed, was again empty but for that same RV, which she now noticed was missing a wheel. The RV had a long-suffering bearing to it, like a worn-down statue in a town square.

The dashed lines of the highway lanes seemed very white, the sun bouncing hard off the wet road. The drive felt shorter than she remembered, the city appearing sooner than expected, enveloping her, making her a part of it again.

• • •

As soon as Eleanor walked into her old apartment, she was struck by how good it smelled, a thought she hadn't had about it once in the seven years she'd lived there. A riotous blend of smells, different notes coming to the forefront and fading again, all of them pleasant. A warm, savory smell, like a pot of soup on the stove, fresh bread being torn open, onions and garlic hitting hot oil. Clean laundry, a just-opened tin of coffee. An orange being sliced, releasing its oils into the air. Lele's hand lotion. The menthol analgesic cream that Lele had used before only morphine would do.

Eleanor felt she was being guided by a gentle pressure at her back to the bedroom, where the mattress was bare—she'd taken the bedding in the first round—and a comforting tiredness overtook her. She was safe now. She could relax.

The closet contained only Lele's clothes, as she'd already brought nearly all of her own to the new house. She pulled a random armful from the hangers, lay down on the stripped bed with the pants and shirts and dresses piled on top of her, pressed over her face. She fell into a black, dreamless sleep.

A fire truck siren racing past the building woke her a few hours later. One of Lele's thick acrylic sweaters felt scratchy against her cheek, loose fibers tickling the inside of her nose. She felt cold. She wondered if she would ever feel warm again.

Going through what remained in the apartment, she found she didn't really need or want any of it. Her rickety furniture and accumulated papers, Lele's kitchen gadgets and tiny clothes. Apparently everything important had fit in her car the first time. She bagged up all the smaller things for donation or trash.

She ran into her landlord on the stairs as she was shuttling bags down to the garbage room. She had lost track of the days, but she knew it wasn't Sunday evening or Monday morning, the only times they were supposed to take out trash; she expected he would lecture her about it.

"Eleanor, I'm glad I caught you," he said. "I sent you a couple emails, but you didn't respond."

Her landlord signed emails and her lease renewals with just his initials, VK, so that was how she thought of him. VK was younger than her, a fact she'd always resented, and owned several buildings in the neighborhood. His excessively neat, angular beard and sideburns looked as though he'd shaved the edges five minutes ago against a ruler, and he wore a waistcoat over a tweed sweater, which made him look even younger, like a teenager in his grandfather's clothes. "It's been a busy couple of days," she said.

"I wanted to say I'm sorry again for your loss. Your mother was always so nice to me."

Eleanor squinted at him. She'd forgotten that Lele liked VK. Eleanor rarely had cause to speak to him—he had a handyman who dealt with complaints, eventually, and Lele had set up the rent to be automatically paid online—but she recalled letting Lele in, one Sunday, after Lele had talked to VK in the hall. "What a lovely young man," she'd enthused. "So polite, so tidy and well-dressed." She'd given him the cookies she'd brought for Eleanor. According to Lele, the rent was a steal, though it had gone up 10 percent every year, and Lele ascribed a moral quality to this, as though VK were magnanimous for letting Eleanor live there at all. "You're very lucky," she'd said. "You have no idea how a landlord can make your life hell."

"Thank you," Eleanor said.

"I was wondering if you would consider ending your lease a little early. I've gotten a lot of interest in the unit. I'll even prorate the days for this month, if you can clear out in the next few weeks."

He was smiling, but there was a hungry glint in his eye. People must be fighting to pay a lot more than she currently was for the apartment. "I might be able to do that," she said. She should have leapt at the opportunity to save three months' rent, but she instead felt a grasping, protective instinct, like something was being stolen from her. Until recently, while still living in the apartment, she'd often found herself staring at the door like she was expecting someone. A knock. She anticipated the knock so hard sometimes she thought she heard it, a cheerful rapping on the wood. And on the other side, she knew, would stand Lele, alive, her twiggy form unbothered by heavy bags of repurposed food containers—stewed beef and turnips in a margarine tub, mapo tofu labeled as yogurt—as on any other Sunday. She had never been sick, never sold her house, never left her job, never asked Eleanor to burn a notebook or act as witness on a DNR or hoard pills, never asked her to watch as Lele writhed and sweated and bit sores on the inside of her mouth. Her mother, the saint. It had all been some terrible misunderstanding. If Eleanor left the apartment for good, then that knock would never come.

She thought again of the locksmith, the check she'd just signed, the missing awning, the leaking windows. "I can definitely do that if you give me my damage deposit back," she said.

He continued to smile with his mouth. "Well, that would depend on how your final inspection goes. If I have to replace the flooring and the blinds, that's basically the whole deposit. And the place was professionally cleaned and sanitized before you moved in, so you can either arrange to have that done yourself, or I can deduct that from your deposit too."

The speckled, squishy linoleum had peeled and scratched over the years, visibly worn along the paths she habitually walked, and the cord on the white slatted blinds had broken off in her hand a few months ago. She wondered if VK had already been inside and seen all of that, or if that happened to every apartment in the building. "If you give me my deposit and refund this month's rent, I'll leave today," she said.

His unsmiling eyes scanned the air, left and right, as he did the math. "Deal," he said.

• • •

Eleanor checked the swing gate for some hidden mechanism that made it shut on its own, and found nothing. Rust continued to eat at the plain, painted hinges. Maybe it was just gravity, a slight slope that pulled it closed under its own weight, or the wind, funneled through this tunnel of trees. When Eleanor got back into the car, Lele was dead in the passenger seat. She'd lost her coat, and the too-tight seat belt seemed to indent her sunken chest.

"Mom," she said, to no one, to the puttering of the engine, "was Aunt Cece right? Were you in your right mind? I just did what you told me to do. I did everything you told me to do."

Lele turned her head the little she could, strapped as tightly into the seat as into a straitjacket, and looked out the window. *It's raining again*, she said.

10

After Eleanor returned from the apartment for the last time, she checked all the windows. The ones at the front and back of the house were all letting in water: On the entryway wall and the back wall of the kitchen, there were seeping dark lines on the floor that were cold to the touch. On the second floor, the smaller window at the top of the stairway landing and the window in her bedroom, the one she'd hoped she'd fixed, were worse—she could only think of them as weeping, like a sacred statue, thin rivulets running on the inside of the glass. The modernist windows had no casing or trim, sitting in a recess of drywall that was too narrow for a bucket, so she wadded rolled-up towels against them.

As she lay in bed that night, rain clattered on the skylight, the sound like a cabinet of dishes in an earthquake. The room smelled wet—the mineral smell of wet rocks, the oily, nutty smell of wet, dirty clothes. She tried to think about how large and comfortable the bed was, willing herself to sleep, but thought instead of the man who built it, how the lumber was shaped and joined by his dead hands. She thought of the locksmith, the man glaring at her at the bar.

She had driven out this way the year before, early in her mother's illness, a day Lele was feeling more or less perfectly well. Aunt Cece had wanted to see the famous mountains. They'd passed Bering Rock without notice and stopped for gas at a later exit. The gas station was also the town post office and sold souvenirs and ice cream by the scoop, a quaint all-in-one building at a four-way crossing. The road east and west led to and from the highway, the road to the north led up a cliffside dotted with houses, and to the south was a viewpoint—a strip of parking poised on a bluff over a wide, picturesque river.

Cece headed inside the gas station as Eleanor filled the tank. Lele had stayed sitting in the front seat, her face hidden behind the reflections on the windshield. "Watch your mother," Cece said, as she passed.

Eleanor felt confused and alarmed by this remark. Why would her mother need to be watched? She watched the numbers tick slowly up on the gauge. She was more alarmed when, after returning the nozzle, she found that Lele was no longer in the car.

Eleanor ran out to the intersection, looking in each direction: highway entrance, town, lookout, highway exit. More than anything else, she felt a child's fear of getting in trouble with Aunt Cece. *Watch your mother.* She'd failed at such a simple assignment.

On instinct, she headed on foot to the right, to the viewpoint. She'd guessed correctly. Her mother's small figure blended into the stunted trees lining the overlook. She stood stooped among them, peering down over the edge.

"Mom," Eleanor called. Lele did not turn. Joining her, Eleanor struggled to sound indignant, as she thought she should. "What are you doing?"

Lele's gaze stayed on the river below, fast-moving, ruffling the reeds and pounding the rocks, molten silver in the light. "I just wanted to stretch my legs," she said, eventually.

"Why didn't you tell us where you were going? Aunt Cece told me to watch you."

Lele peeled her eyes away from the drop at last, turning to Eleanor. She smiled and looped her arm through Eleanor's. "To watch *me*? You?"

Eleanor leaned against her mother. They laughed quietly, heads close. "I know," Eleanor said.

• • •

Eleanor rose from bed, walked out to the landing and down the stairs. On the entryway floor, beneath the wooden chandelier, there now lay an oriental rug, the deep red of its medallion pattern faded, indented by the footed university bookshelves. The parts of her front door lockset were spread out across it.

Richie stood in the middle of the room, holding half of the splayed-open lock, wiping it with a rag. *You're going to be third author*, he said. *You and I both know you deserve to be second, but Dr. Kenney would pitch a fit. It's all politics, my dear.*

"I'm honored," Eleanor said, reaching the bottom step. Her hand released the railing. "Truly."

Richie looked her up and down. *Isn't that what you were wearing yesterday?*

She'd had this conversation before. She dutifully recited her lines. "It didn't make sense to go home while my tests were still running."

I've seen you sleeping under the desks in the lab. You look like a little girl when you're asleep.

Eleanor flushed, as she had the first time. "I won't do it again."

That's not what I meant. Richie put down the piece in his hand, picked up another. *I admire your dedication. But perhaps your colleagues would appreciate it if you went home and showered occasionally.*

She knelt on the rug before him. She raised her eyes without lifting her head. Richie's body stretched upward. He grew taller as she watched—the ceiling rose steadily with him, until both were as high as the forest canopy outside, his face looming like a moon. His arms and legs lengthened out of proportion with his head and torso, first like a gangly teenager, then into a stringy, inhuman shape. The rug fibers, stiff with decades of dust, scratched at her bare knees and shins.

Do you live far? the giant asked.

"No. I take the number 40. Just one bus."

I live just past the east side of campus. Ten-minute walk. You're welcome to use my place to freshen up, in a pinch. Take a shower.

"The student gym is closer," she said, as though that made sense, as though anything about this conversation made sense, then or now.

Richie-Culver held the door handle and rag in one hand, tiny alien trinkets in the vastness of his palm. He reached for her face with the other hand, his arm stretching more to cross the distance, muscles and flesh thinning and distending like putty. *Think of me like family,* he said, one warped fingertip brushing her cheek. *Whatever you need to get your best work done, let me know. That's what I'm here for.*

• • •

Eleanor was back in bed, her eyelids weighted and crusted over, sticking as she pulled them apart.

She rolled onto her feet. She walked out to the landing, to the top of the stairs. Again. She thought of how, in grad school—another phase of her life marked by insomnia and strange waking hours—she had often dreamed of getting out of bed, taking a shower, brushing her teeth, getting dressed, packing a sandwich, only to wake up and realize she had to do it all again. She would sometimes then do none of it, shuffling to the lab with her winter coat over her pajamas, her teeth fuzzy and her breath stale, crashing out between banks of computers as they all did, all obsessed with their work, with Culver's career-making approval. Until that day he'd told her how vulnerable and innocent she looked while she slept.

The entryway, below her, appeared empty and dark. She could make out the wooden bench if she strained. No bookshelf, no rug, no monstrously sized creature lying in wait.

She called out for Lele. The room remained empty, the darkness without form.

11

The heavy rain continued for four days. Eleanor felt trapped indoors, imprisoned by the rain, the changing rhythm keeping her awake at night. In a single hour, the rain would patter like nervous fingernails on a desk, then rapidly increase in tempo—a building drumroll—until the downpour roared like a waterfall, the sky ripped open above. Ebbing again, unleashing again, a noisy melodrama that she couldn't ignore, that never faded into the background.

The weather abated on the fifth day around dawn, fine droplets of rain hanging in the air like mist. Eleanor hiked up the slope at the back of the development land to the office trailer and its ever-shining light. Lele had bought Eleanor the boots she wore all the time, expensive and waterproof with deep treads when they were new, but now worn slick at the bottom, holes opening along the stitching between the uppers and the soles.

She knocked on the door. She tested the handle and found it unlocked. She pushed open the door without stepping inside, letting it swing.

The office had been torn apart. A love seat in the style of the chairs in her living room, the same wood frame under disconnected cushions, had been ripped open, the stuffing pulled out and soiled by some small nesting creature. An upholstered desk chair on casters had met the same fate. A mini fridge lay on its side, the door hanging off its hinges, the rubber casing of its electrical cord chewed through. A dead rat or squirrel, decomposed past meaningful difference, lay on top of a space heater, what remained of its front paws and nose dangling over the front edge. Only the desk, pushed up against the wall under the window, seemed relatively unscathed. Here and there, in the beige gray and blackened green of mold and debris, dots of bright color stood out: a crushed soda can, a blue hard hat, and a single red-and-white sneaker, also shredded and gnawed away. All of this had happened since March.

The light came from a bare bulb hanging from the ceiling, the cord clipped along the top edge of the wall. She followed the line of it with her eyes. The switch, nonsensically, was on the far side of the room from the door. The land developer would have had to feel his way through the dark trailer each day to turn it on, and exit in darkness at the end of the day after flicking it off.

She'd come to turn off the light. The sight of it from her house, the yellow square at the base of the mountain, made her feel watched, like someone was in here. She'd seen no cars, no one coming or going, but still the light bothered her—she knew it would go on bothering her, even having seen the state the office was in, confirmed it was unoccupied. But she couldn't bring herself to go in. She feared electrocution and tetanus, and some vaguer evil. The stink of death, the frailty of human monuments.

She shut the door and turned back. In the valley below, the water pooling in the empty housing sites was milky and opaque. Her house, where she'd left the lights on, glowed like a distress beacon, permeable to eyes and rain. The windowless second-floor bathroom had become her favorite room, the only place she felt comfortably alone, where she didn't feel seen without seeing.

She unlocked her front door, slipping her hand under the garbage bag. Already the lock was slightly stickier than before. She wondered why the office had been so thoroughly infested while her house had been pristine when she first saw it, why nature had left it alone.

Seeing inside the office had given the land developer a new solidity, made him feel more present, imbued the other house and the construction portable with a renewed, brooding energy. She could picture the office as it had been, with the furniture upright and intact. She saw him sitting at the desk, looking out over the site and the army of workmen. He appeared in her mind as a figure from another time, a conqueror of a bygone age—pioneer, land baron of the Old West. To early colonizers, nature must have seemed a formidable, indefatigable enemy, one you could blast away at forever without consequence. A river too large and powerful a thing to poison, a mountain too ancient and gigantic to erode, the seasons and weather divinely ordained. She imagined his face: a black push-broom mustache, slitted eyes, round pink cheeks. A smug, well-fed mien.

She tried not to imagine his face blown apart.

She headed up the stairs, to the window at the top of the landing. The reflection of the clouds, brisk sails in the wind, shifted the light on the corresponding window on the other house, at the top of *his* stairs, like a flash of movement. Or perhaps it was movement: animals who had eaten their way through the walls, seeking shelter from the rain, nesting in the insulation and nibbling on the wires and whatever had been left behind. Perhaps, in contrast to her house—the model home, stately in its emptiness—his house was crammed with the contents of the bigger home he'd been forced to give up, furniture and junk piled to the ceiling, now a warren of mice, rats, opossum, raccoons. Perhaps he had prepared for a long siege, filled the cabinets with food, and now they swarmed and seethed with vermin.

She imagined the cleanup after he shot himself. The first officer on the scene, a local boy, back at the bar with everyone else, describing it to a leering crowd the same way the cashier had, fingers under his chin. *Right here.*

She had left her bed unmade, the bedroom door ajar. Lele's ghost had not appeared in days. Eleanor went looking for her at night, leaving every door and closet open, checking over her shoulder, searching the space around her reflection in mirrors, listening for voices in the clamoring rain and wind. As hard as Eleanor resisted the thought, the dead rodent reminded her of Lele. The images merged in her mind—the rat on the space heater, Lele beside her in the bed. Something in the unnatural stillness, the deflated, abandoned look of the body, like the molted shell of a crab.

• • •

At ten a.m., a woman from the curtains and blinds company Matt had recommended arrived. The rain had picked up again. She carried a blue-and-white-striped umbrella that looked like it was made to shade an entire family at the beach. She didn't ask about the garbage bag taped to the front door as she introduced herself from under the umbrella. "Jaclyn," she said. Her hair was clipped in the back with styled bangs, her nails manicured but short. She wore a frilly buttoned cardigan under a sensible fleece. Eleanor felt like she'd met her before, then realized she closely resembled Mary, her real estate agent before Matt. This woman overwrote Mary in her mind. She would forget what Mary looked like, would only see Jaclyn in those memories from now on.

Jaclyn left her umbrella outside, leaning against the wall by the door. She walked through each room with a measuring tape as Eleanor scurried after her. "Your house is so beautiful," she gushed. "So much light!" She snapped the tape away from herself in quick, practiced motions, like a trick artist with a whip. She said nothing about the creep of moisture under the first-floor windows, the wedged towels on the second floor. "I'll have my guys take more precise measurements later, of course. This is just so we can do a quick estimate."

They sat down together at the dining table, and Jaclyn encouraged Eleanor to pore over binders of fabric samples. She held a swatch up to the light to demonstrate its opacity. "How much is that one?" Eleanor asked.

"Let's pick out what you like best, first, and then I'll calculate it all out, and we can adjust from there—there are a lot of factors. Do you want electronic controls? Are we doing the skylights as well?"

While typing vigorously on a tablet computer she'd brought, she said, "My guys can come to measure this week. Being custom, the blinds will take a couple months to manufacture, and then we'll get you on the schedule for installation. We can probably do everything by March." She tapped one more time with her index finger. "There we go. How does that look to you?"

She turned the tablet to Eleanor. The total was over $20,000. Seeing Eleanor's expression, Jaclyn said, "We could remove the blackout layer in the bedrooms, if you'd like to save a little there."

"Not to put too fine a point on it," Eleanor said, once she'd found her voice, "what would the cheapest option be? Just to get all the windows covered?"

Jaclyn pursed her lips, caught herself, smiled again. "Give me a second." After a few minutes of wordless clicking on the screen, she said, "I can get it down to $8,200. But you'd be sacrificing a lot."

Eleanor stood from the table. "Can you email that estimate to me, and I'll think about it and get back to you?"

"I'll email them both to you so you can compare," Jaclyn said. "Feel free to send me any questions. I'm sure we can find a balance somewhere in the middle, where you can get some of what you want within your budget."

Eleanor thanked Jaclyn and showed her out. Once the windows were fixed, she thought, she would tack sheets over them.

Matt's recommended contractor, Kurt, arrived that afternoon. He had shoulder-length, curly blond hair tucked under a baseball cap, a way of looking around the room rather than at Eleanor as they talked. Though she hadn't acquired a pair of men's shoes, she wore a costume ring she'd found in the apartment junk drawer on her last visit, on her left ring finger. Kurt only grunted in acknowledgment as she showed him each of the leaking windows. He asked no questions, personal or otherwise, so her fictional husband never came up.

"Could be a lot of things," he said, at last. "I can't really tell without cutting into the wall. You're in luck, though. Usually we schedule a few months out, especially since there's so much work right now, with the rain. But we finished a project early this week, so I have some guys I can bring in right away. Tomorrow at eight a.m. work for you?"

"I'll be here, but I'll be working. There will be blocks of time when I can't be disturbed."

"That's fine."

She felt better after Kurt left. He seemed unalarmed, like the leak was a problem that could be easily diagnosed and immediately solved. She had an intuitive sense that the windows could not wait, but she could save up for the awning later, maybe even the blinds in the long run. She felt lucky that she wouldn't have to continue to change and wring the towels for months, watching the line of water lengthen across the floor. Better still, she felt like it was out of her hands. Someone else would take care of it, take care of her.

12

Eleanor met Teddy and Mira for dinner that night. The couple had chosen a restaurant overlooking the harbor that Eleanor thought of as a place only tourists went. As she walked in, the wraparound views of the sea were overshadowed by the worn-down maroon carpeting and chintzy pillars, the dimness and drapery that felt more oppressive than glamorous. A grand piano took up its own split-level to one side, the gloss dulled by dust, a handwritten card reading DO NOT TOUCH perched on the key cover. The empty fish tanks built into the wall separating the kitchen from the dining room seemed particularly bleak—the dead water backgrounded by an unnatural blue, the last working filter burbling mournfully.

There was no one at the host stand. Eleanor saw Mira sitting alone at a table against the far glass wall, staring out at the marina, the rain, the sky crowded with naked masts. She didn't want to be alone with Mira, without Teddy. But there was no way to avoid it. They greeted each other, and Eleanor sat in the facing seat.

"Theo's coming from the office," Mira said. Her bob was stark, box-dye black. She had heavy lashes and the kind of faded blue eyes that appear almost colorless. She wore a shapeless dress of black crepe, black leather driving loafers, and four gold necklaces layered down her chest. At the tables behind her, families dressed in sweatpants, leggings, fleece vests, and mud-crusted sneakers shared baskets of fried fish and clams. Eleanor wore one of her plain, dingy sweaters, over blue jeans worn white at the crotch and knees. Mira was younger than Teddy, Eleanor knew, so much younger that—as he'd put it—it had *caused a stir* when they first got together. "But then she joined me in the realm of the middle-aged," he'd said, "and then the truly aged, and it hardly mattered anymore. We outlived judgment."

Mira gestured to the dregs of her cocktail, a sprig of rosemary drowning in ice. "The drink special," she said. "I wouldn't recommend it. I was about to switch to white. I'll get a bottle for the table."

"I drove." Eleanor had resolved not to drink.

Mira stared at her.

"So I should only have one glass," Eleanor added, weakly.

Mira nodded. She tracked a server with her eyes. "I have so much I want to ask you," she said, which struck Eleanor as ominous. "Why has it been so long?"

"I guess since we gave up the old office, Ted—Theo—Dr. Mitchell and I didn't do a good job at staying in touch," Eleanor said.

Mira was leaning far back in her chair. She smiled. "You don't actually call him 'Dr. Mitchell.'"

"No. I don't know why I said that." Eleanor wiped her palms, suddenly damp, on the thighs of her jeans. "How long *has* it been? Since we last saw each other?"

"Four years, I think. You were at our anniversary party. The last party we threw before the pandemic."

"Right. Of course."

"While I was waiting," Mira said, "I was trying to think of how we first met. When Theo introduced us. I can't seem to remember. Was it a dinner like this? Or did you come to the house?"

"I don't remember either," Eleanor said.

"I know he'd known you for at least a couple of years," Mira said, still smiling. "He was keeping you from me."

"I don't think—" And then Eleanor remembered. Slowly, she said, "You came to the office. That's where we met."

Teddy arrived. Neither of them had noticed him entering the restaurant or walking in their direction. "Hello, ladies." He kissed Mira on the cheek and sat on her side of the table. He rubbed his hands together in mock excitement. "I'm starving. What are we having?"

"I haven't looked yet," Eleanor said.

"There's an oyster platter," Mira said. "Twelve oysters, four varieties. We could start with that."

Eleanor glanced down at the words *market price*. "I don't really like oysters. But you guys go ahead."

"Our waiter has been circling that family of ten nonstop. I can't seem to catch his attention," Mira said. To Eleanor, she added, "Theo doesn't usually take clients on Mondays. He went all the way downtown for just one appointment. Who was it, darling? Someone important?"

Teddy glanced at Eleanor, smiling nervously. "You know I can't tell you that, dear." He busied himself with the menu. "Yes, let's do the oysters. And, oh, the nicer of the Rieslings."

"Of course you can," Mira said. "Not by name, not specifics. But the gist of it. You always tell me. It was the CFO, wasn't it? The embezzler?"

"Mira," Teddy said, sharply. "We're in public."

"Eleanor, I want to get your opinion. I *know* Theo is allowed to tell you. That's just called consulting, right? You used to consult him about your clients all the time."

In the limited encounters they'd had, Eleanor had found Mira intimidating but compelling—blunt and self-possessed, with an arch, wry way of speaking, such that everything she said sounded deathly serious and like a joke at the same time. But tonight she seemed slightly off-kilter, unmoored, careening in her gestures. She had worked as an account executive in ad sales for a newspaper, back when the city had two major papers instead of one. Since they'd last seen each other, her paper had gone under, after being sold three times in three years and a brief online-only stint, and Eleanor wasn't sure what Mira did now. "That's not exactly—" Eleanor began.

"Okay, fine," Mira interrupted. "Then let me ask you a *hypothetical* question. Hypothetical questions are allowed, right?"

Eleanor glanced again at Teddy. His mouth was set in a line. "Sure," Eleanor said, finally.

"When would you break confidentiality? Hypothetically."

"What do you mean?" Eleanor said.

"Like, you have to report a client who tells you they're beating their child, yes?"

"Oh. Yes, we do. By law."

"Or if they're abusing their disabled grandmother?"

"Dependent adults, yes."

"When else?"

"If they were at imminent risk of suicide. If they had a plan, and the means, and I believed they were about to immediately carry out that plan."

"You would tell the authorities, in that case. An involuntary hold, say."

Dr. Culver had also liked Socratic lines of questioning in his seminars. Eleanor remembered this sense of precarity, balancing on your back foot, the frantic calculation as you tried to figure out what he wanted you to say. Wilting under his gaze. How you tended to believe an opinion when he'd guided you into saying it yourself. "If it was absolutely necessary for their safety," she said.

"What if they were plotting a murder?"

The waiter interrupted. Mira ordered the oysters, the wine, an appetizer of seared tuna, spring pea risotto; Teddy got the squid ink pasta. Eleanor had just enough time to skim the top of the broadsheet-sized menu and choose the cheapest of the salads. As soon as the server stepped away, Eleanor said, "I would ask them why they'd come to see me, why they were telling me, what they were hoping I could do for them. I would assume they're seeking help. They want help with managing those—thoughts, and don't want to enact them."

"But if they did end up murdering someone, wouldn't you feel responsible? Wouldn't you regret not reporting them when you had the chance?"

Eleanor looked at Teddy, expecting him to jump in. He loved these kinds of arguments. He continued to stare at the tablecloth. "The thought is not a crime," Eleanor said. "There's likely nothing the police would do. All that would accomplish is scaring someone away from therapy, from speaking openly and asking for help, who needed it desperately. I would tell them that if it rose to the level of a crime, an immediate threat, like, 'I bought a gun and I'm going to do it tonight,' then I would probably have to report it. I would tell them that early on—I might make it a condition of our working together. I would first probably encourage them to turn themselves in."

This might have been true five years ago, Eleanor thought, if this hypothetical client were across from her in those leather armchairs, in the hush of the office she'd shared with Teddy, the whole of their person trembling, troubled, earnest. A decade ago, she might have given this exact answer in a bar with her undergraduate classmates, pompous baby philosopher kings, all. This was the kind of therapist they'd all aspired to be. Today she would turn the client away, terminate the relationship with a faceless, bloodless click of her mouse, a canned pop-up. Toss the would-be murderer back into the sea of moaning, desperate digital ghosts.

"Teddy said he wouldn't even report someone who already *had* murdered someone," Mira said.

"What I said," Teddy rejoined, quietly, "was that if someone told me they'd murdered someone *a long time ago*, and in my estimation, they were not about to do it again, there was no immediate danger to any real, specific person, I see no reason to break confidentiality."

"You would take on that client," Mira said.

"Maybe. If I thought I was the right fit for them. If I thought I could help them process that experience, or with whatever they had come to me about."

They were interrupted again by the ritual of the wine. Mira's slight nod of approval, three glasses filled, the wine almost clear, the faintest wash of yellow. "What if," Mira began, seemingly enjoying herself, relishing her own words, "they were abusing their disabled grandma in a nonphysical way? What if they were stealing from her?"

"Again," Eleanor said, "why are they telling me about it? I assume because they want to stop. They want to change themselves or their circumstances so that they wouldn't have to steal, so they could resist the temptation."

"Why is physical abuse the hard, bright line? And not financial abuse?"

"That's what the law says," Teddy said.

Mira turned in her seat to face him. "So you wouldn't report physical abuse if you didn't have to?"

Teddy lifted his wineglass and turned it, watching the liquid catch the sides, as though the answer to her question lay within it. "I probably would. But maybe not. It might be more of a judgment call, case by case, as to what would be best for all parties. Involving the authorities might only make things worse, in some cases."

"You think you know what's best for all parties. You know better than the exploited grandma," Mira said, "about what's best for her and what she deserves to know."

"I certainly wouldn't break confidentiality to contact *her*," Teddy said. "That would definitely get me sued, cost me my license."

"But you'd know you did the right thing."

"I don't know that I would. Do you not understand what my job *is*?"

"You mean you think you could fix the thief."

"I don't 'fix' people, Mira. But I do think—"

Mira turned back to Eleanor, cutting Teddy off. "What if your client was manipulating Grandma, tricking her into giving him *all* her money? Leaving her destitute, unable to meet her basic needs? Isn't that a kind of physical abuse, if she's going to be homeless and starving?"

Eleanor had been looking forward to this dinner, since Teddy had texted to invite her, on behalf of himself and Mira. Mira's presence allowed Eleanor to recast his parting kiss as paternal, to return him to the father-mentor figure she wanted him to be. She'd wanted to tell them about the house, to ask for their advice, had imagined their reassurance. "Oh, the windows on our summer cottage leak every winter," Teddy might have said. "It's nothing to worry about." She wanted them to share in her horror over Richie, to ask them about money. "That's just what custom blinds cost, I'm afraid," Mira might have said, or, "Highway robbery. That woman is trying to scam you." Her image of them, after all these years apart, had worn away at the edges, turned them into generic elders, eager to dispense wisdom, generous from their established position in the world. She imagined Mira saying, "If the work on your place gets to be too much, you're welcome to stay with us."

She saw now, in this moment, she was nothing to them. A pawn, a prop, a witness. A minor character in the ongoing drama of their life together.

"My responsibility is to my client. Confidentiality is the bedrock of our relationship. It's not my place to judge them or predict the future." Eleanor had the sense she was repeating someone else's words; there was a split second when she heard her voice and wasn't certain who had spoken, her or Teddy. Where had she heard this, phrased exactly this way? Teddy looked pleased.

Two servers appeared at Eleanor's elbow, bearing two trays full of food. Eleanor pushed her chair back slightly and leaned away from the table, giving them room to lay out the plates, the large platter of oysters nestled in ice. Mira scowled. To the servers' retreating backs, she said, "Why would they bring all the food at once? They didn't ask. My risotto will be cold by the time we've gotten through the appetizers."

Teddy squeezed a lemon wedge over the oysters, a pip flying across the table and landing on the carpet. Eleanor watched Mira and Teddy each toss back an oyster from its cleaved housing, the flesh slithering out of the shell, a trickle of fluid catching Teddy on the chin. They had begun with the largest variety; in her narrow, sunken face, Mira's cheeks bulged as she chewed, her lips forced out into a pout. Eleanor was goaded into taking a thin slice of tuna, which was oddly pallid and flavorless, the color of underripe watermelon at the center, eraser-shaving gray at the edges, a vague, vanishing meaty sensation on her tongue.

Mira swallowed her third oyster, took a long drink of wine, and then picked up the conversation again. "So we are unmoved by the plight of the single grandma," she began.

"The harm doesn't outweigh your need to reform the sinner, or whatever."

"For fuck's sake, Mira," Teddy said. "We're not missionaries."

Mira waved this away. "How many grandmas does it take? Are we moved by a hundred grandmas? A thousand?"

Eleanor bit into one of the shrimp from her salad, trying to ignore the strong, fishy odor. It crumbled softly to the tooth, like feta cheese. A wave of nausea rose up her back. She suppressed a retch and managed to say, "I don't understand what you're asking."

"Let's say your client confesses to swindling hundreds of people. Thousands of people. Stealing their retirement funds, their savings accounts, their pensions. Many of them—what was it?—*dependent adults*. Confused old people."

"How could you possibly know that?" Teddy snapped. The squid ink had already stained the plaque on his front teeth black.

"It's a reasonable inference. What then? Would you report them?"

Eleanor hadn't read the description of her salad. Whole, indelicate leaves of radicchio and endive were tossed in a mustard dressing, bracingly bitter and sharp. She couldn't help imagining a child at this table, faced with these odors and textures, the sour wine, the slick briny oysters, the absence of any easy, accessible pleasures. She imagined herself as a child, kicking her feet under the table, chin just above the level of the tablecloth, gazing longingly at the other tables and their heaps of french fries. "Report them to whom?" she said.

"An anonymous tip," Mira said, rolling her wrist to suggest this was just occurring to her now. The spoon in her other hand pierced the surface of her congealing risotto with a grotesque, bodily squelch. "To, I don't know, the FBI. The SEC."

"The SEC? Why the SEC?"

"Mira, that's enough," Teddy said, aggressively rolling a large ball of noodles onto his fork, the color suggestive of poison. "This is unbelievably inappropriate."

"What? It's a hypothetical question. A consultation with one of your colleagues." Mira looked directly into Eleanor's eyes, as though shutting Teddy out, removing him from her field of view. "Would you keep taking his money?"

Teddy let his fork clatter to the plate. "You think that's the worst thing a client has ever told me?" he said harshly. "You think that's the darkest secret I've kept? You think all my other clients made their fortunes from what, planting trees? Feeding starving children?"

When they had shared an office, Teddy had charged triple what Eleanor had, which was still—approximately, it was harder to say, given the virtual platform's ever-shifting deductions and method of calculating her hours—double what she made now. She felt foolish that she had never really considered what difference that would make in terms of the clients he drew. She'd thought it was a matter of experience, that she would charge just as much someday. And the consultations had always gone in one direction. She'd asked for his opinions, and he'd never asked for hers. She remembered walking up Teddy and Mira's long drive for their anniversary party, on the eastern edge of the city, at the lakeshore. The brick house at the end was tall and stately, the walk lined with lush flowering hedges and weeping cherry trees, the early buds shriveled and red before they could flower.

She remembered, too, the first time she'd seen Mira. In their old office, in addition to the two white leather armchairs—which Eleanor always used for her sessions—there was a third, mismatching chair in green leather set off to the side, which Teddy used for clients he thought would benefit from not being faced directly, and a chaise longue against the wall.

The chaise was a relic, a kind of in-joke of an analyst couch. The facing wall was lined with bookshelves, and an imposing oak desk with a leather mat where Teddy did his charting; Eleanor mostly did her paperwork at home.

She had been lying on the chaise longue, and Teddy was sitting at the desk, chatting during a lunchtime crossover—she was done with the office for the morning, and he had clients in the afternoon and evening. She could even remember what she was wearing: a collared, black-and-white, calf-length polka-dot dress and a white cardigan, the dress dowdy, even matronly, when she was standing or sitting in the armchair, notepad in reach. But when she sprawled on the chaise, the hem rode up above her bare knees, and the loose neck spread, the air on her collarbones. She had been gazing up at the ceiling, not at Teddy, though she knew he was watching her from the desk, and that he was doing nothing else—he had no files, nothing in his hands. He was only looking at her, only listening. They had been talking about Antoni, whom she had recently begun seeing, who had filled her with a new sense of ease in the world, with whom she thought she might already be falling in love.

"I'm happy for you, E," Teddy had said. "It sometimes seems like you don't have a lot going on, besides work. And you have to be mindful about the toll this work takes, the weight of other people's stress and pain. You have to notice when it gets to be too much."

"How can I tell?"

"Oh, you know the answer to that. The usual effects of secondary trauma."

She rolled her eyes. "How does it manifest for you?"

Teddy didn't answer right away. "Clients are always telling me their dreams, no matter how much I discourage it," he said, finally. "When it gets really bad, sometimes I dream their dreams."

"And what should I do, if it gets really bad?"

"Seek therapeutic help yourself. Perhaps from a trusted colleague." Teddy's voice was lower than usual, somber, overly enunciated like a radio announcer's. His therapy voice. She giggled, luxuriating in talking freely to someone she couldn't see, their self-aware playacting at her being his client. She stretched her arms over her head, feeling her body elongating, the dress tightening across her chest. "Take a vacation," Teddy continued. "Maybe with this new boyfriend. Get some much-needed *recreation*."

They had not locked the door from the small waiting room—why would they? Teddy wasn't expecting a client for hours. At the sound of the door opening, Eleanor's head popped up like a groundhog. She leaned her body on one elbow, her dress twisted, the neckline askew. She squinted at the shape in the doorway. The overhead lights in the antechamber seemed as bright as a surgical theater compared to the dim office, where they'd kept the blinds down and the lamps off, sitting and lying in the sleepy afternoon.

Mira stood there. Eleanor knew at once she was Teddy's wife. The angular bob, the watercolor blue eyes.

Eleanor and Teddy weren't touching. They were on opposite sides of the room. But Eleanor saw the guilty expression on Teddy's face, his hands slack in his lap, a sheen of sweat on his forehead. And she knew suddenly that there was something untoward about this, something subtle, about the analyst couch, about the power in Teddy looking at her and Eleanor not looking back.

The one vestige of luxury the restaurant retained was the thickness of the glass wall, the building's insulation from the rest of the world. Outside, the boats in the marina rocked against one another like toys in a bathtub, and in the orange pools beneath each dock light, heavy rain made the water roil. The decorative trees along the waterfront walk dipped and swayed, their upper branches nearly touching the ground. But the scene played through the glass as though on a muted television. And despite the occasional screech or wail of the tourist children, the dining room had a hushed quality, voices drowned in the carpet and lost to the high, vaulted roof.

Teddy, therefore, ranting now about Mira's hypocritical, inconsistent moral compass, his face gathering blotchy color, was causing a scene. Mira interjected coolly at intervals—"You can't pretend this isn't extraordinary, like you counsel crooks of this magnitude every day," and "That's different. It just is," and "You wouldn't be so upset if you didn't think I was right."

Eventually, Teddy became aware of other diners glancing at him over their shoulders, and he sputtered out, sinking into his chair. In the void left behind by his voice, the attention of Eleanor and the other diners was drawn to something outside the vast, screenlike window. A man was walking on the waterfront against the wind, forcing his way forward, step by step, his body at a hard slant, blocking his face with the inside of his elbow. He was soaked to the skin in a hoodless trench coat. He looked like a mime or a silent film actor, the wind too extreme to be anything but a fiction.

"I'm going for a smoke," Teddy said, sulkily.

Mira gestured at the drenched man, who was slowly rounding the corner.

Teddy stood up. "There's a covered area out by the entrance."

When he'd gone, and the two women were alone with the spread of cold food and shells, Eleanor expected Mira to apologize. On Teddy's behalf, or for both of them. Instead she refilled her wine, sipped at it, and stared appraisingly at Eleanor, until Eleanor was the one to break the silence. "So Theo is smoking again," she said.

"Now and again. He got fatalistic in the early days of lockdown, convinced he wouldn't live to see the end of it, so he might as well enjoy himself."

"I can understand that." Eleanor looked away from Mira's steady eye contact and pressed the side of her fork into a shrimp on her salad. It smeared formlessly, like pâté, and she felt queasy again. She thought of the land developer's office, the dead rat, the blooms and domes of mold.

After a thoughtful pause, Mira said, "Is Theo a good therapist? In your estimation. I've always wondered."

"I don't know how to answer that. He charges a lot and never seems to want for clients, so he must have a good reputation, and they must be happy with their outcomes. Especially these days, with online ratings. He was a good mentor to me."

"Did you ever sleep with him?"

Eleanor jolted. Mira's expression had not changed. "No," she said. "God, no."

"It honestly doesn't matter to me. I used to feel so sorry for you—rescued from Michael by Theo, of all people."

Eleanor felt her face tighten. Teddy didn't rescue her, she wanted to say. Lele did. "I didn't need rescuing," she said, instead. "I needed someone to supervise my licensing hours."

"And then you never sued Michael or accused him outside of the kangaroo court of the university. You let it all go."

Eleanor's eyes went unfocused. The shrimp on her salad blurred, broken-backed curls of pale pink, slick with dressing, wriggling as though alive. "It wouldn't have accomplished anything," she heard herself say. "I wanted to move on."

Mira took a long swallow of wine. She picked up a piece of tuna on her fork, where it hung limply like a tongue. "Theo's not a bad man," she said. "Not like Michael. He's just . . . weak. He wants things to be easy and pleasant and how he likes them all the time. He uses therapy-speak to justify total moral relativism. Everything is abstract to him."

Eleanor thought of her client, David. "We're all just doing our best in a compromised world."

"That's exactly what Theo would say. What a good student you are."

Eleanor's ears were hot. "I bought a house," she said, abruptly. The sentence had been on the tip of her tongue all night, waiting for a moment that never came. She just wanted to change the subject. She felt gratified that Mira looked so surprised.

"Congratulations," Mira said. "How?"

"What do you mean?"

"How did you afford it? Who would give you a mortgage?" Reading the offense in Eleanor's expression, she added, "I don't mean to insult you. My nephew and his wife are trying to buy a house right now, and they are having a hell of a time getting a loan, in part because he's self-employed, like you."

"My mom left me enough for a large down payment."

"Ah," Mira said, drawing out the syllable, like that explained everything, more than the original question. "I'm sorry for your loss. I remember you brought your mother to our anniversary party. That unexpectedly final party."

"I did?" The memory rewrote itself suddenly: Lele holding Eleanor's arm as they walked up the drive, Lele admiring the landscaping, Lele the one who explained the sickly-looking flowers on the cherry trees. "You'll have a house like this one day," she'd said.

"You did. She was so sweet. And smart. Sharp as a tack." Mira tilted her empty wineglass into her mouth, shaking out the last drops. "Is it true she did your laundry for you? Cooked all your meals?"

Mira didn't seem angry, or mocking—her expression was flat, mildly curious, as though she had come upon a strange-looking insect. I'm not real to her, Eleanor thought. I'm not a real person.

"That must have been a terrible shock," Mira continued, without waiting for an answer, "to go from being so coddled to so alone. Did you have to learn how to use the washing machine? How to turn on the stove?"

Eleanor remembered, one afternoon, bringing a basket up from the laundry room in her apartment building. She had overstuffed the dryer, and despite feeding it quarters to run for hours, she had opened the machine to find the wad of sheets and blankets still wet, the pillowcases balled up inside the duvet cover. When Eleanor returned, frustrated and apologetic—she couldn't even do this one goddamn thing—Aunt Cece was sweeping up a plate her mother had thrown. Lele was still trying to yell from where she lay on the couch, her voice weak and hoarse. "Don't give those vultures any more of my money. They know I'm going to die. They're just trying to bleed as much out of us as they can before I do." Cece had looked up, taken in Eleanor's basket of soggy linens, and sighed.

Eleanor had come tonight wanting to be pitied as the helpless child she was, and now that it had happened, she hated Mira for it.

Teddy returned, his white hair damp and deflated, the front of his shirt and pants speckled with rain, carrying the smell of smoke. He appeared to be in better spirits. "It's wild out there. Took me forever just to get the damn thing lit," he said.

"Let's get the check," Eleanor said. "I want to get on the road before the weather gets any worse."

Teddy shook his head. "I can't imagine how it could get worse."

• • •

The city lights in her rearview mirror disappeared quickly. There were mercifully few cars on the highway, as the downpour picked up and she could hardly see a car length in front of her. The featurelessness of this highway—infinitely repeating lines on asphalt and the dark, infinite fields of scrub on either side, the way you could be anywhere in America—might have represented adventure to another kind of person, she thought. The open road. But Eleanor felt a fear that grew with each mile of emptiness, like she was driving farther and farther into an abyss, the light and civilization ever farther behind.

As she started down the main road through Bering Rock, the church bell rang, the sound distorted and half swallowed by the wind. The dashboard clock read 8:48 p.m., an utterly illogical time for bells. What service could be ending, what call for prayer, what hour marked? She counted each peal. She reached twenty, still able to hear it, as she made the turn onto the mountain road. It occurred to her that she had never heard the bell before. Her house was too far for the sound to carry.

She passed a cluster of three deer, sheltering beneath the trees by the roadside, unblinking, still as statues. On the day they'd gone to show Cece the mountains, Cece had spotted a deer, excitedly pointing it out through the back window. Lele and Eleanor had exchanged an amused, indulgent look.

Is it true she did your laundry for you?

The swing gate was open. She heard Lele as soon as she passed, though she couldn't see her, the voice strengthening as it spoke. The voice came from just over her right shoulder, as though Lele were in the middle back seat, leaning forward. *They're horrible people*, the ghost said. *Mira and Teddy. Horrible. Why should you care what they think?*

It was the first time Lele had come to her in several days, since the day she'd given up the apartment. She felt such relief that her hands slackened on the wheel. The car drifted left before she righted it again. "Mom," she said, aloud. "You're back."

But she remembered the real Lele now, in Mira and Teddy's crowded kitchen, as Teddy poured champagne into two dozen flutes that were lined up on the counter. Teddy had looked flushed and happy, in his element as host. Eleanor had been alone on the built-in banquette in the corner, and she'd watched her mother talking to Mira on the opposite side of the room, both of them laughing. She remembered her surprise. She wouldn't have expected them to get along. This memory was hazed in golden light, the early evening through the French doors, or just the tint of all her memories from Before. In the Before, Mira and Teddy had had a certain grace, a kind of worldly sophistication and detachment and ease. They were not always horrible. Eleanor was almost sure of it.

• • •

Eleanor rose from bed, walked out to the landing, down the stairs. She found the dining table covered in computers. Each monitor was painfully bright yet did nothing to illuminate the dark room, haloed with no shadows. The machines were arranged edge to edge, as many as could fit around the perimeter of the table, screens facing outward. Every screen displayed a person—a low-quality video call, a stuttering image of a human head facing out into the room, dotted with pixelated artifacts. Their individual voices were soft but loud in aggregate, chattering unintelligibly like birds.

This time, when she emerged from the dream, finding herself back in bed, when she called out for Lele, she was there. She sat at the foot of the bed, facing away from Eleanor, the hair at the back of her head patchy and gray, the orange flowers spilling down her spine. Lele stood and made her way to the bedroom door without ever showing her face, her back always to Eleanor, her steps stately and measured. She continued out of the room. Through the doorway, Eleanor watched her drift silently to the dream stairs, where at the bottom the computers had waited, the giant and the red rug. Eleanor was too afraid to follow.

13

Kurt was late the next morning. They arrived at 9:55, and Eleanor had client appointments at ten and eleven. "Van had some trouble on the mountain road," Kurt said. He'd brought two other men, one of them disconcertingly young-looking. He could have been a boy of thirteen or fourteen.

"That's fine," Eleanor replied hurriedly, her mind on the session for which she was already late. As she explained that she would be unavailable for the next couple of hours, he held out a metal clipboard. She hesitated at the sight of the tight text on carbon paper.

"This just says you're allowing us to investigate the cause of the leak, and you agree to pay the day rate for three guys," Kurt explained. "You're not committing to the work or any estimate yet."

Kurt's air of authority and the impersonal flatness to the way he spoke—as though only ever stating facts, the absence of charm or persuasion—made her want to trust him. She signed and dashed upstairs, leaving the men alone in her entryway.

She had moved two dining chairs into the spare bedroom. She sat on one and propped her laptop on a box on the other.

She thought she had an existing client at ten and an intake session at eleven, but opening the platform, she saw the order was reversed. She was now ten minutes late joining the call and couldn't remember anything about the new person.

"Good morning"—Eleanor glanced at the display name—"Wendy. I'm so sorry I'm late. There were some circumstances beyond my control." Her voice echoed in the empty room. Eleanor was distracted by the small image of herself in the corner. She was lit only by the window behind her, darkened by rain, and the camera compensated for the lack of light by blowing out her features, her eyes and nostrils black holes bored into a pale mask. Her face was puffy from lack of sleep, softening the lines of her cheeks and jaw. She looked like her mother.

The much larger face on the screen frowned. "Wing-Yen," she corrected.

"Oh, my apologies. It says Wendy on my end."

"Yeah, that's . . . I don't know how to change that."

As Jaclyn had resembled Mary, Wing-Yen looked familiar, and Eleanor eventually recognized that she looked like another former client, someone who had simply not scheduled a sixth appointment, fading away without comment or complaint. Everyone was beginning to resemble everyone else to Eleanor.

"So," Wing-Yen said, after a moment, "how does this work?"

"Well, why don't we begin with what brings you to therapy?"

Wing-Yen frowned again. "It's a requirement for visitation with my daughter. We messaged about this. That's why I picked you."

"Right, yes. Of course." Eleanor clicked through her files, pulling up the scanned Parenting Plan that had been attached to Wing-Yen's profile. Three boxes were checked—*Neglect, Child abuse - physical, and Emotional or physical problem*—but the child abuse box had been scribbled over, the correction initialed by a mediator in pen. The daughter, Shannon, was two years old. "Again, I apologize. It's been a frantic morning. Um, the evaluation line is blank—"

"My ex-husband requested I undergo some kind of counseling before seeing Shannon again. I agreed voluntarily. It's just to make him feel better. He's paying for it. We can just sit here in silence for ten sessions, if it's all the same to you. As long as you sign the compliance report."

Eleanor chose to smile blandly, as though Wing-Yen were joking. "If we're going to be here anyway, we might as well talk. How long were you married?"

"Eight years."

"Do you think you would benefit from counseling?"

Wing-Yen was slow to answer each time she spoke. Eleanor couldn't tell if she was suspicious of Eleanor, cautious of the words she used, or just a thoughtful and serious person. Or if the connection was lagging. "I'm not sure."

"Why do you think it was important to—" She glanced at the Parenting Plan again. "Calvin, right? Why do you think it was important to him that you seek counseling?"

Wing-Yen had a markedly blank expression. "He would have to answer that."

Eleanor waited, hoping Wing-Yen would fill the silence, but she continued to stare impassively into the camera. Eleanor skimmed Wing-Yen's profile in a side window as surreptitiously as she could. Her occupation was listed as unemployed. "I asked what *you* thought his concerns were," she said, gently.

Eleanor waited longer this time, meeting Wing-Yen's hollow gaze through the screen. When she finally spoke, it was at such length, in such detail, as though reading a prepared deposition, that Eleanor couldn't hide her surprise, the eyebrows on the little face in the corner shooting up.

"Calvin went back to work four weeks after Shannon was born. The first day I was home alone with her, I said goodbye to Calvin at the door, early in the morning, and sat down in an armchair in the living room. Shannon had just eaten, and she fell asleep in my arms. I remember I could see her eyes move through her eyelids, they were still so thin. Ostrich—our dog—lay at my feet. I remember there was a lamp left on, on the other side of the room.

"And then all of a sudden, Calvin was shaking me, his hands on my shoulders. He was screaming. The baby was screaming, and stinking, and wet. I was still clutching her to me. The dog was cowering in the corner by the door, having peed on the rug. It was evening. The lamp was still on."

"Were you assessed for postpartum depression?"

Wing-Yen looked disappointed, as though Eleanor were a student who'd asked a revealingly stupid question. "My doctor said I should get more sleep."

"I see. Did you continue to have episodes like this?"

Wing-Yen shook her head. "No. Not exactly. I learned to focus on just the most important things. Feeding the baby, changing her diaper, keeping her safe from harm. Dumping food in the dog's bowl, letting him out into the back garden. Everything else could slide."

Eleanor felt like this story was sapping the energy from Wing-Yen, her blinking slowing, like she was falling asleep telling it. "What wasn't important?"

Again the considered pause, the precise, high diction. "Feeding, bathing, or dressing myself. Dressing Shannon—it was summer, I didn't see why she couldn't just wear a diaper. Entertaining or disciplining the dog. Laundry, dishes. Housework of any kind. I ordered more and more burp cloths and bottles on the internet, left it to Calvin to sterilize whatever he thought needed sterilizing."

Eleanor felt it was best just to let her keep talking. She made a sympathetic face, but Wing-Yen seemed to be staring past her, into the fiber-optic void. "Before I was a mother, I wouldn't have said I was a particularly messy person. Calvin and I kept a tidy home, and maintained the illusion of an even cleaner one when friends or family came over. But after the first time you just let a wadded-up tissue fall from your hand, wherever it may land, it's easier to do it again. And how that becomes an ocean of garbage, washing wall to wall in the short hours your husband is away, becomes hard to explain when he asks. Hard to explain to someone who wasn't there." She dropped her voice, mimicking her husband. "'Why? Why couldn't you just put it in the bin, two steps away?'

"I told him the dog destroyed the sofa while I was in the other room with Shannon, but that wasn't true. Shannon was alone in her crib when it happened. I stood in the hallway, at the threshold to the living room, watching as Ostrich tore into the first of the cushions. He buried his muzzle in the split and shook the shredded foam stuffing loose, all over the room." Wing-Yen gestured wildly, mimicking the dog's motions with her hand, but her voice stayed flat, her eyes emotionless. "Shannon was crying. Her crying was so pure, so abject, like nothing I'd ever heard before. She cried like she wasn't just hungry but like she had never been full. Like she had never been fed and never would be, like she was the last creature alive on earth. I listened to Shannon cry and watched Ostrich eat the couch and couldn't take a step toward either of them."

Eleanor waited to see if Wing-Yen would continue. "Did Calvin take over when he was home? At night, on the weekend? Did you ever get a break?"

Another long pause. Wing-Yen's dead-eyed stare. "I experienced Calvin as an interruption," she said, at last. "A naive emissary from the world outside. Shannon and I lived in the now, the unrelenting present, whatever she needed right this instant. Whereas Calvin cared about the past. He wanted to know how many times she ate, what volume of formula, how long she'd slept, how many minutes passed between feedings, between diapers. Questions I couldn't answer. Data I didn't record. He cared about the future, about gifting her a world of colors, shapes, and textures, filling her ears with words, placing her on her stomach and cheering her on like a personal trainer. To Calvin, there was still a meaningful difference between night and day, the sun still a greater authority than Shannon, some reason not to hide behind blackout shades in the midafternoon or turn on every light in the kitchen at two a.m. 'She's bigger today,' he'd say, and I couldn't explain that she was bigger with every passing moment, like a tumor, like a dying star.

"And the mess was not a mess when Calvin wasn't there. It was just the way things were. The absence of order was a kind of order, of harmony. A towel crusted in spit-up didn't *belong* in the hamper any more than it belonged anywhere else—on the sofa, on the floor, in the freezer. The towel simply existed. Whenever he tried to clean, it made things worse. By putting a few things away, he restored every other object to its state of shame and displacement. He would trip over a box of diapers in the hallway, find a plastic teething giraffe inside his pillowcase, a stick of butter with a bite taken out of it on top of the toilet tank, and he'd ask, 'Why is this here? Why is this here?' But why not there? Why is anything anywhere?"

There came a flurry of banging from downstairs, the whirring and grinding of power tools. Eleanor could tell that Wing-Yen heard it, on her end of the call, saw her startled out of the reverie of her speech. "I'm sorry about the noise," Eleanor said. "And I'm sorry you didn't have the support you needed, during that difficult first phase of parenthood."

Wing-Yen's mouth twitched. A grimace, a wry smile. "Do you have kids?"

"No, I don't." Wing-Yen nodded knowingly, as though Eleanor wore her childlessness on her face. "So this—the state of the house, the catatonia—was the basis of his neglect claim?"

"No, that was later." Wing-Yen looked down, as though she had to concentrate to remember what she wanted to say. "Calvin had put Shannon on a wait list for this insanely expensive day care near his office. He filled out the paperwork before she was born, as soon as I was in my second trimester. Her spot on the list was coming up, and he was up for a promotion, with a raise, so we could just about afford it. He was convinced this would fix everything. I could go back to work. I could go back to who I was before we had her. He was frustrated that I wasn't more excited. More grateful. I just couldn't imagine it. It was like trying to imagine being someone else. Like he was telling me I'd wake up tomorrow in the body of a stranger."

The racket from below ceased. In the sudden quiet, Eleanor could hear a faint hissing from Wing-Yen's microphone. Her breath, the ambient noise of wherever she was. "Did he get the promotion? Were you able to secure her day care spot?"

"Yes."

The muffled conversation of the workmen rose up the stairs. "But something else happened first?" Eleanor supplied.

"Calvin says he came home and found the front door open and unlocked. I probably received some packages, dragged them inside, and didn't close the door properly. He says he called my name and I didn't answer, but he heard splashing in the bathroom. So he went to the bathroom, and I'd left that door open too.

"Calvin says I was sitting in a filled bathtub, fully clothed. Shannon was naked in my arms, resting on my belly. He says my hair was wet, and my eyes were closed, and the water was cold."

Eleanor wanted to ask: Where were Shannon's grandparents, aunts, uncles, cousins? Where were Calvin and Wing-Yen's friends and neighbors? But she knew the answer. There was only the day care, and now Eleanor, paid to play their roles. "You don't remember?" Eleanor said.

"Maybe she had a blowout diaper and I decided to bathe her in the middle of the day," Wing-Yen went on, as though Eleanor hadn't spoken. "Shannon hated the bath chair we used. She would scream as soon as she felt the slick plastic under her. I can imagine why I would have just gotten in with her."

"You don't remember," Eleanor said, mostly to herself.

"I don't know why I didn't undress. I don't know why the front door was open. I don't know how long we were in there, if at some point the water had been warm.

"I *think* I remember Calvin taking Shannon, wrapping her in a towel, rocking her. I can hear him saying, 'She could have drowned,' over and over, but I don't know if it was right then, or later, when that phrase became the chorus of our lives, when it became all he ever said to me.

"Sometimes I think that I could have stopped it all if I'd reacted the right way, in the moment. If I'd thrown myself to the ground, lamented what a terrible mother I was, begged for forgiveness. But as Calvin tells it, I stayed in the bathtub, reaching for Shannon, as though trying to take her back. And then, eventually, *she could have drowned* became *you tried to drown her*."

"But you didn't." Eleanor did not intend to say this; it slipped out.

Wing-Yen turned to the camera, her eyes still empty and faraway. "My mother asked me that," she said. "'You didn't do it, right? You can tell me.' She's suspicious because I agreed to the Parenting Plan that Calvin drew up, and because I'm letting him move out of state with Shannon and his new girlfriend.

'You didn't fight,' my mom said. 'The courts would be on your side, *if* you really didn't do anything.'"

Wing-Yen leaned forward an inch, a gesture so small that it might have been imperceptible in real life, but because the top of her head now blocked the overhead light behind her in the video frame, the feed faltered, adjusting, her skin tinting yellow and green before resettling at a sickly gray. "What does it say about me that the person who gave me life, and the person I vowed to spend my life with, both believe I'm capable of murdering my child?"

Eleanor gave in to an impulse to touch the screen, near the bottom, below the horizon of the camera, where Wing-Yen wouldn't see. As though she could put her hand on Wing-Yen's shoulder, and they each wouldn't be alone.

• • •

After her second session, Eleanor checked her phone and saw a text from Kurt: *pls come talk when avail.*

As soon as she opened the bedroom door, she found that the hallway landing was noticeably colder. Had they turned off the heat? She followed the sound of voices to the kitchen. "Rutting season," one of the men was saying. "Bucks will be going wild."

"Good luck to you. I don't hunt anymore," Kurt replied.

"Why's that?"

"My daughter is against it."

A snort. "She eat meat?"

The third man: "Your daughter tells you what to do now?"

The house seemed to grow colder as the voices grew louder. She hadn't intentionally quieted her steps, but when she walked into the kitchen, all three of the men jumped. Kurt was leaning back against the counter, empty-handed, and the other two were sitting across from him at the island, each eating a foil-wrapped burrito.

The window on the back wall was gone.

Eleanor was so mesmerized by the size of the hole—two-thirds of the wall, floor to ceiling—and the openness it created, the intrusion of the outside, like she *was* outside, the bracing air and unveiled sky, that it took her a moment to see the removed window leaning against the adjacent wall, blocking the walkway behind the island. The edges of the hole and window itself both looked ragged, as though they'd been unwillingly torn apart.

"The boys were just taking lunch," Kurt said. "They can eat in the van, if you prefer."

As though the burritos were what was strange about the scene. "That's okay," she managed to say. "What—what's going on with the window?"

"Well, I have some bad news." Kurt stepped through the hole, and this too seemed incredible. He walked through the wall of her kitchen. He gestured for Eleanor to follow, but unlike Kurt and his men, she wasn't wearing shoes. She ran to the entryway and returned in her tattered boots and jacket, feeling the eyes of the other two as they glumly tore at their food.

The wind made a low keening sound, like someone wailing in the distance. Rain beaded on Kurt's baseball cap and ponytail, stippled a continent-shaped puddle on the gravel strip between the house and where the woods began.

She pushed up her hood and joined Kurt. Seeing the house from this angle, she stifled a gasp. They had removed a large portion of the siding from the outside wall of the kitchen, the boards piled on the ground by the hole, raindrops drumming upon the loose wood.

"The weather barrier under your siding isn't the right type," he said, speaking loudly to be heard, "and even if it was, it's not installed correctly. You'll have to rewrap and re-side the whole house to stop the water from getting in."

"How much will that cost?"

"It's hard to say exactly. I'd have to price the materials, and I didn't expect we'd need to be here so long, so the schedule is tricky too. The siding itself is so new, maybe we can salvage it, but it's been just soaking in water on the underside. Optimistically, I'd say around fifty, sixty thousand."

Eleanor didn't respond right away. Her bizarrely multicolored kitchen, from the outside—the icy water dripping down off the front of her hood, still reaching the tip of her nose, her eyelashes—looked warmly lit and inviting, starkly different from its surroundings, midday cast in a timeless gloom, the darkened mountains and flooded homesites. The hole in the wall looked like a portal to another dimension.

"Your home insurance might cover it," Kurt said. "We'll close this up for today, and I'll get you a better estimate to give to them."

The two workmen inside were talking. She could see their mouths moving but couldn't hear what they were saying. The young one, who had looked to Eleanor like a teenager, seemed even smaller from this vantage point, his feet dangling from the handmade wooden barstool, his back thin and hunched. The older one was dominating the conversation with an authoritative air, but not like Kurt's. Shakier, bossier. He seemed to be shouting, but not *at* the boy, who seemed unfazed. Ranting, monologuing, fury without direction. He stomped his foot for emphasis.

And then Eleanor realized the boy was not a boy but an old woman, the small form at the island beloved and familiar, in those same pajamas—the pajamas that gloved strangers had stripped efficiently away, maneuvering her mother's nude body like a plank of wood, rolling her into the zippered mouth of a bag while Eleanor stood to the side, her face pressed into the wall.

And the other man, she knew him too. In the unadorned, austere beauty of her furniture, in the unending light burning on the hillside. It was the man she'd made up, the pioneer: the mustache and the slitted eyes and fleshy cheeks she had invented. He looked back at her, through the hole. The top of his head was gone, above the eyebrows, the shattered skull and tangled nest of brain and flesh visible but contained, as though he wore a tight-fitting cap of gore.

"Ma'am?"

Eleanor turned back to Kurt, her vision blurred with rain. What would she tell a client to do? She focused on the logo on Kurt's baseball cap, then the shirt collar peeking past his gray windbreaker, then the stubble on his neck, the stiff bristles moving with the skin as he breathed, darker than the hair on his head, and finally the concern in his eyes—for her, or for himself, but real, human, alive.

"Why don't you head back inside and give your insurance company a call, and we'll get back to work?" he said.

Eleanor felt relieved to have instructions. Marching orders. Lele would have liked Kurt, she thought, just as she had liked VK, her former landlord. A reasonable man. She'd also said that about her oncologist, whereas Eleanor and Cece had found him infuriating, his uselessness and false promises. "He didn't give me cancer," Lele had said. "You don't shoot the messenger."

Eleanor and Kurt reentered the kitchen. The two men nodded at her as she passed.

14

Cloistered again in the empty bedroom, Eleanor found her policy paperwork as an email attachment from Vance, the mortgage broker, and did what Kurt had told her to do. She put her phone beside her on speaker, playing the crackling, tinny hold music, a technology that had seemingly never improved in her lifetime.

She had to hang up after an hour, as she had an appointment with a client. "You're somewhere different again," Kristy said.

"I'm just in another room," Eleanor replied. "How are you? How was your week?"

"Good, actually."

"I'm glad to hear that." Eleanor checked her notes. "How many stickers did you put on your calendar?"

"What? Oh, I'm not doing that anymore. I have big news." Kristy straightened in her seat. The video quality was better than the two that morning, per the whims of the telecom gods. Wing-Yen had sat close to the camera, her skin flatly colored and textureless, the neckline of her fuzzy sweater a muddied blur. Kristy wore a gray hoodie, and Eleanor could clearly see a bleach stain over the breast, a dirty-white slash about two inches long, like a stab wound. Eleanor knew this hoodie, and that Kristy spent exorbitantly on clothes that Eleanor never saw, that she very possibly never wore. "I've decided I'm not going to buy anything for a whole year."

She waited for Eleanor to react. "That's very ambitious," Eleanor said, after a moment. "What brought this on?"

"I've been watching vlogs of people who've done it. It's called a no-buy year. Or a savings sprint. And it's—what it sounds like. No clothes, makeup, accessories, skin care, home goods, takeout, coffee. Nothing. Just the bare essentials for a whole year. Just making do with what you have. It's amazing. It's beautiful to watch. They save so much money, and they find themselves, and learn about what they really need. It's like their brains are rewired."

Kristy beamed expectantly. She was thirty-four, but she felt younger to Eleanor, something dogged and hopeful in her that Eleanor associated with youth, with an endless number of days ahead, endless versions of yourself you could become.

"I have no doubt that would have a positive effect on one's brain chemistry," Eleanor said, carefully. "And I would be happy to support you through such a project. But that's a lot of change and restraint all at once. I wonder if we might break it down a little bit, start with something smaller and more achievable, so you could experience some success right away. Perhaps a no-buy week, or we could revisit your plan from last week, with the wish list and the stickers. There's a lot of research to suggest that—"

"No," Kristy said. "I need to go big, and I need to go cold turkey. I've already started preparing."

"Preparing? Preparing how?"

"You know, buying last-minute stuff. Enough shampoo and conditioner and skin care products to last the year. And I'm going to a wedding in April, so I had to buy a dress and shoes for that, and a dress I can wear to any holiday parties. And Christmas and birthday presents for Lee, and my nieces and nephews, and my parents, and Lee's parents."

Loud hammering came from below, and then a sharp yell from Kurt, and the hammering ceased. Murmured, urgent conversation passed between the men, loud enough to carry through the house, and then the banging resumed. "Is that everything you bought this week?" Eleanor said.

"Well, I had to get backups of stuff that will wear out over the year—underwear, socks, tights, bras, running shoes, winter boots. And a better coffee machine, and a milk frother, and a better kitchen knife, and a Dutch oven, since I won't be getting coffee and takeout. That kind of thing. So I won't have to shop during my year and be tempted."

Something about having two chairs in the center of the room made the empty space feel larger, made the walls feel distant. Still cautious, Eleanor said, "Kristy, may I ask—how did you buy all of this at once? I thought your cards were maxed out."

"Not quite. I had to spread it across a few. And I used those buy now, pay later apps, staggered out over the next few months, since I won't be spending the rest of the year. There's no interest if you make the payments on time."

The despair Eleanor felt caught her off guard. She thought she'd grown hard-hearted to Kristy. She looked so happy, the improved video quality showing even the white-blond baby hairs frizzing off the sides of her face. "I see," she said, at last. "You know, I was thinking—it's been a while since we talked about you possibly seeing a financial planner."

"I looked into it. They're *so* expensive. And a lot of them seem like scams, to be honest. And this is obviously more of a psychological problem than a financial one, right?"

"I don't disagree with that. But sometimes we need . . . more people on our team. The same way, if you were having physical symptoms, or needed pharmacological support, we would involve a medical doctor or a psychiatrist. I'm not suggesting you replace our sessions with a financial planner, but there are parts of this situation that might—"

"I looked into it," Kristy repeated. "But you're way cheaper."

Eleanor thought of Teddy's resistance to doing sessions online. She did wish she were with Kristy, right now, that she could shove herself into the screen and emerge on the other side, step out of Kristy's computer and into her home, her life, to drag her unopened packages from their hiding places. Eleanor inexplicably wanted to smell Kristy, to feel the radiant heat of her body, to know the true, unfiltered colors of her features. To see, for the first time ever, Kristy's legs and feet. She wanted to hold her, to bind her arms to her sides, to shake her.

Past her screen, Eleanor became aware of a row of people standing against the far, blank wall, lined up, spaced so their shoulders didn't touch. Their expressions were patient, expectant, looking in different directions, as though they were waiting together for a train. Lele stood out as the shortest among them, the land developer beside her. The rest were all clients. Wing-Yen and David stood in the far corners, and an empty space in the middle fit her computer from this perspective, where they'd left room for Kristy. But her clients were alive. They had families and jobs, could still brush against strangers on the sidewalk, could still share a warm bed with a lover. Why did she imagine them as lonely and isolated as the dead?

• • •

After her last session of the day, Eleanor came down the stairs just as the two nameless workmen were leaving through the front door. Kurt appeared behind them. "Good timing," he said. "We're done for the day. Did you get in touch with your insurance company?"

"No. I called them whenever I was between—meetings, but I never got through."

"Well, keep trying. You could file online, but in my experience, nobody will get back to you in a hurry that way. Especially not right now. I'll email you an invoice for today and an estimate for the wrap and siding." Kurt was already on the other side of the door, his hand on the garbage-bag-wrapped handle.

"Wait," Eleanor said.

He paused but did not turn back. She didn't know what she wanted to ask, only that it felt too soon for him to leave. "Um, thank you," she said, lamely.

He gave a curt nod of acknowledgment and closed the door behind him. She heard his van's engine starting up outside as she walked toward the strange, milky light coming from the kitchen.

Plywood boards had been nailed across the top and bottom of the hole where the window used to be. A translucent plastic sheet was stapled to the plywood. It flexed noisily in the wind, like Foley thunder, as the pressure inside and out competed—taut and concave, then taut and convex, like a lung.

She didn't know what she'd expected. That they would put the window and siding back, restore the house to the state it was in this morning, with its slow, ignorable leak.

Her phone pinged. Kurt had already emailed her the invoice, seemingly from the van, before her house was out of sight. Three men, day rate, a diagnostic hole in the wall: $2,500.

• • •

Eleanor ate her last hot dog, mandarin orange, peanut butter sandwich, and boiled egg, as the plastic sheeting strained like a sail in her peripheral vision. She hadn't eaten all day, wary of going into the kitchen while the crew was there. She sat with the hold music for another two hours before someone answered. She gave her information, repeated what Kurt had told her about the weather barrier and the siding.

"I can submit your claim, and we can send an agent out," the voice on the other end said, "but I can tell you right now, your policy doesn't cover faulty workmanship, only acts of god."

"Isn't the rain an act of god?"

"Based on what you just said, in your contractor's estimation, the problem isn't the rain. It's the construction of your house. I see you're the second owner, and the house was built this year. Under state law, the building envelope warranty is five years. You shouldn't be calling us. You should be suing the builder."

"He's dead."

Without reaction, without missing a beat: "His company or estate, then. Or possibly his siding subcontractor. Our agents are extremely overloaded at the moment, and this doesn't sound like an emergency, and is almost definitely going to be denied. I recommend you consult a lawyer."

"I—" Eleanor had what she knew was a ridiculous impulse: to ask this person to recommend a lawyer. To better explain how to sue the man who bankrupted and then shot himself in the house across the road. To tell her more specifically what to do next. To hold her and cook her a hot meal and tuck her into bed. *Can't you see*, she wanted to beg, *that I'm stupid and helpless and alone?* "Okay," she said.

"Have a nice evening."

• • •

She texted Matt several paragraphs, troubled when he didn't respond right away, as he always had. She turned off the heat in every room except her bedroom and the upstairs bathroom, where she cranked it high—with the missing wall, it seemed a futile battle, like she was trying to heat the outdoors, the whole world. She took a long, scalding shower. The chill she felt was so consuming, so total, like her blood was slush, too frozen to travel through her veins. Her skin went pink, then red, and still she felt cold. The sound of the water striking the tiles—how she had loved the extravagantly tiled room, when she first saw it—sounded too much like the rain, beating down upon the house from all sides. An invading force, overpowering her house's feeble defenses.

She dressed in layers, shut herself up in the bedroom, and stuffed more towels against the base of the door to keep the heat in. She wrapped herself tightly in the blankets. She left the lights on. The wind seemed to rock the whole building, the rain astonishingly loud on the glass, like flung rocks. She had figured out the rattling in the kitchen came from the exhaust fan over the stove—something must have been broken or loose inside, where the passage was open to the wind.

Around two in the morning, there came another of those moments of respite, a noticeable calm. The dying of the wind, the rain thinning, not quite sputtering out.

In the sudden silence, the metallic chugging of the wall heater on full blast seemed loud and insistent. Between the heat and the rain-saturated towels in the window, the air in the room was humid as a sauna. She felt choked by it, flashes of hot and cold through her body, as with a fever.

You just have to promise not to give me the pills until then. Even if I beg. Even if it seems like I've changed my mind.

She rose from bed, walked to the landing, and looked through the weeping window into the other house. The land developer stood in his window, in that subtle jut that protected the front door, the one her house didn't have. His head was intact. He toyed with his mustache, tugging just above the center of his upper lip.

He'd already made a fortune in real estate, the cashier had said. *Millionaire* did not suffice, for even the incomplete, terraforming work done to the valley: to level and tame the forest, to line the basin of the valley with concrete and gravel, to connect to water and power at such distance, to build civilization from scratch. Richer than god. Enough money for a lifetime, several lifetimes, if he'd just known when to quit. Lele had recognized in VK—Eleanor's landlord—forgivable greed, human in scale, but this would have been something grander, hoarding ruinously as a dragon.

She had another seven a.m. appointment with David, who feared he lived in a sandcastle. She lived in a model house, a stage set, an illusion to impress investors. Perhaps the house across the street was a *real* house, the components chosen and assembled with care by someone who actually intended to live there. To be sheltered for a lifetime rather than dazzled for a moment, panicking as a cavalcade of luxury cars came rushing down the hill, cash in hand.

She continued through the house without turning on the lights. She walked out the front door in her socks, through the ankle-deep water of her walkway, across the gravel road. The clouds had never cleared enough for her to see the stars.

The land in his front yard sloped gently away from the house, the rain running into the neighboring plots. She tried the door and found it locked. She could break in, she thought, and no one would care. Smash a window and no one would hear.

He stood in the same window, watching her from above.

"I'm supposed to sue you," she called.

He smiled crookedly, with irony, as if to say: *Many have tried.*

15

Eleanor considered taking her first appointment from bed, but couldn't bring herself to sink that low. She needed her clients. She dragged the dining chairs from the spare bedroom into hers, resealed the door with the towels. The white walls of her bedroom now gleamed faintly with moisture, like a sheen of sweat.

"Good morning, David," she said.

"Morning."

David was a skittering human shape, lurching from frame to frame, his glasses melted into his face like raccoon markings. A pop-up warned that the call quality was so weak, she should consider switching to audio only. "Can you hear me okay?" she asked.

"Yeah, you sound fine. I was kind of expecting you to cancel."

"You were?"

"Yeah . . . I guess you weren't affected by the storm?"

Eleanor didn't know how to respond. She hadn't thought of it as a storm, which sounded like something that began and ended, a disaster potent and brief. The heavy rain had gone on and on for weeks, and every break felt temporary, a glimpse between sheets of water sweeping across the land, never enough time for anything to drain or dry. The day she'd gone to her old apartment was the last time the rain had eased for more than an hour.

"Sorry, am I allowed to ask that? Is that too personal?"

"No, of course you can ask. I'm doing . . . fine. Are you and your wife okay?"

David laughed—a short, incredulous honk. "Yes. We're totally fine. It's the craziest thing. We live at the bottom of a hill, and literally everyone up the hill from us lost power three nights ago. All the streets higher than ours, and even the other side of our street. My wife was letting people come in to charge their phones and use the microwave. The power just came back this morning. For us, it was almost kind of . . . nice. We've lived here for five years and somehow didn't know any of our neighbors. Is that a psychotic thing to say?"

"No, no. It sounds like you found a feeling of purpose and community."

She couldn't tell if David had winced at her response, or if his face had just glitched on the way to its next permutation. "I was worried at first that people would—I don't know what. Rob us? Demand to stay the night? Run up our electricity bill? We live in a—what do they call it? A mixed-income neighborhood. I sound like such a jackass. I am a jackass. Everyone was nice, even apologetic. And I'm not the one who went out to talk to people in the street in the rain, who went knocking on doors. That was all Jeanie—my wife. It hadn't even occurred to me.

"The irony is, I was sitting at my computer, reading about other people who had it even worse. Out by the airport, all those basement apartments that flooded. Four people died. And Oakedale, of course. God."

Eleanor tried to recall why Oakedale sounded familiar. She hadn't been reading the news.

Apparently the connection was good enough for David to identify the searching, confused expression on her face. "The mudslide in Oakedale," he clarified. "I think most people evacuated in time, but a lot of people are still unaccounted for, and the town itself is completely gone. Wiped out."

She remembered then, the picture forming in her mind: the green highway sign she'd passed each time she'd driven from the city. BERING ROCK 2, OAKEDALE 22. Oakedale was only twenty miles to the east.

Was Oakedale where she'd stopped with Cece and Lele, where Lele had run off to the river lookout? The gas station–post office, the colorful little houses built up onto the cliffside, standing out against the steely mountain rock. Ice cream by the scoop.

She should echo David's epiphany back to him. She rooted around in her mind for the words, something about how he'd been empowered by helping his neighbors instead of sitting around doomscrolling. But she wanted to peel back the soggy towels and look out the window, into the valley, at the endless, biblical rain, to see if it had turned to blood or frogs. How could a place so near have washed away without her knowing? All those buildings, all that water and mud—where did it go, where did it end up?

Her first session with David had concluded with his confession of fear. But he did not seem afraid today, not really—he seemed, if anything, relieved. The universe had only affirmed his belief that he was and would remain the luckiest motherfucker around. And wasn't she lucky too? Like David, she hadn't lost power, she hadn't drowned in a basement apartment by the airport, hadn't watched the ground beneath her entire town liquefy.

• • •

After her call with David, her stomach urged her back down to the kitchen. It was after eight now, but nearly as dark as it had been when she'd felt her way through the house five hours earlier. Matt still had not replied to her text. The cold house had a still, anticipatory air that she tried not to disturb, as though someone else were shut up and asleep in another room. As though, beyond the one warm bedroom, she was a trespasser in the rest of the house, an unwelcome guest.

The kitchen was brighter, the east-facing hole giving the room a dim, even glow. The plastic sheet rippled softly between its staples and nails. Wet and backlit, the sheet was almost transparent, but coated in a white haze, like a veil of fog over the blue-black smudges of the mountains. She thought she saw something moving up on the ridge, dashing across the horizon. Deer, most likely, or just an illusion of the wavering sheet. Rutting season.

She stared into the empty fridge. She had no appointments the rest of the day, and only one tomorrow—she should spend some time reviewing and adding to her notes. The only food she had left was a half-empty jar of peanut butter. She took a spoon from the utensil drawer.

At the top of the stairs, she noticed that the glass bowl in the center of the entryway chandelier looked somehow different. It was hard to see, nested within meticulously carved slats of wood, even at eye level from where she stood on the stairway, but where the glass had been spotless and clear, it now looked clouded, streaked with dirt.

It was full of water.

She could not begin to parse what this meant, where the water had come from. Still standing on the stairs, she took her phone from her pocket. Her first thought, as always, was to call Lele. She let her hands scroll toward *Mom* by muscle memory, watching as though they were someone else's hands. She stopped her finger earlier, interrupting herself, in the *K*'s. She paused over Kurt's name.

Lele stood on the landing.

Again, Eleanor was struck by her solidity, the sense that the ghost was more substantive than before. But was that exactly how Lele had looked at the end? Or was Eleanor changing the details as they slipped away from her, slackening Lele's jowls, whittling away her flesh—her eyes huge and shining, dilated black pools—making Lele look sicker, older, more deranged? Sweet, Mira had said. Smart. Sharp as a tack.

Kurt's not your mother, Lele said. *He's a businessman, and you owe him $2,500.*

This Lele could not help, Eleanor knew. This was the one she'd killed.

"You're in luck," Kurt said. Luck, what luck, lucky her. "I'm on my way to a job out sort of your way, a town over from Bering, and traffic seems pretty good. I can stop by after—no, actually, before. Before makes more sense. Is it okay if I come right now?"

"Yes, please," she said, like a child offered ice cream, offered solace.

She sat on the hard stairs and didn't move. She felt Lele watching her. The chandelier was, Eleanor thought, the loveliest of all the wood pieces the dead man had made—more delicate and more intricate than the rest of the furniture. When on, the light was artfully diffused, the shadow of a hundred-legged spider spread across the high ceiling.

She imagined, for a moment, a goldfish spinning through the bowl of the fixture. The glint of scales, tail ephemeral as smoke. She imagined that the lightbulb still worked but cast a cool, blue light that fish could circle unharmed.

• • •

Eleanor only rose when Kurt rang the bell. He arrived alone. She opened the door, and he dipped his head in greeting, stepped inside, and immediately craned his neck to look up at the mounted light. He whistled, the strongest emotional reaction she had seen from him. "Hang on," he said, "I'm going to grab a ladder from the van."

Perched at the top of the ladder, Kurt took from his belt what looked like a long, pointed, serrated knife, a fairy-tale dagger. He stabbed it into the ceiling. Eleanor made an involuntary noise, as though the drywall saw had instead been plunged into her body—a yelp, a half-swallowed cry.

He withdrew the knife. Water gushed out and onto the concrete below.

"Might want to grab a bucket," Kurt said, his voice level.

By the time Eleanor found anything resembling a bucket—a large plastic bowl, still unpacked in the kitchen, that Lele had used to wash vegetables—the water had stopped. A thin layer of water spread across the entryway floor. Kurt had moved some of her shoes out of the way and rolled up the near edge of the living room rug.

"Is it the rain?" she asked, holding the bowl uselessly against her belly. "The weather barrier?"

Kurt shook his head. "What's above the entryway?"

"The bathroom."

"Go and turn on the shower."

She sprinted up the stairs, taking them two at a time, as though speed would make any difference. Before she made it back to the stairwell, Kurt called, "Turn it off!"

He was folding up his ladder when she returned, and the ceiling was dripping again, a few drops at a time, like eaves after the rain has stopped. "I have to get to that other job. I can redo your bathroom for you, eventually, so the shower's not draining into the ceiling, but you're going to want to call a water remediation company first. I'll text you the name of some guys I've worked with in the past. You should see if your home insurance is willing to spring for a hotel room. I think you could argue your house isn't livable."

Lele walked into view on the landing, as though she had emerged from one of the bedrooms. "They won't cover this," Eleanor said. "They're not covering anything."

"Who's your agent? When did he come out?"

"Nobody came out."

Kurt managed to sling the ten-foot ladder over his shoulder. "What did you tell them?"

"What you told me, about the siding and the wrap."

He shook his head. "And they said what? That it should still be under the builder's warranty?"

"Yes."

"And you know who the builder is, right?"

"Yes," she said. Kurt shook his head again. Eleanor asked, "Should I have lied?"

"Of course not," he said, giving her a look that suggested otherwise. "I would never suggest that. That's fraud." He glanced at the ceiling again. "But you don't have to tell them everything. 'My house is flooding. I don't know why.' Let them figure it out, decide what's the fault of the rain and what's not. It's chaos out there right now. Might as well get anything you can out of them, since they're definitely not renewing your policy after this, and it'll be hard to find a company who will. And you have a mortgage?"

"Of course I have a mortgage."

"Well, there you go."

"What do you mean?"

Kurt had taken the few steps to the door, still wearing the ladder as though it were weightless, like a purse. He turned back, opening his mouth to speak, but seeing her expression, he closed it again, apparently deciding against continuing his explanation. *He's not your mother.* Eleanor felt like she was shrinking, sinking into the floor. Like Mira, Kurt could see her for what she was, a stupid and pitiable child, still singing along to the TV show theme in her head: *How does the world work?* "Look," he said, finally, "everything is going to be okay. You figure out the money, and I can fix everything."

In what she supposed was a mercy, he only charged her $200 for the visit.

16

Eleanor used a mop to push as much of the foamy, discolored water out the front door as she could, and then to swipe it around pointlessly, as though cleaning the floor with the filth. Every towel she owned was already in use.

Lele continued to observe from the open landing above. A different voice emerged from Lele's mouth—the customer service representative Eleanor had talked to the night before, blown out by the speakerphone. *Faulty workmanship. Acts of god.* Lele pointed toward the bathroom. *Noncompliance with building code is two years. You should sue him, or the plumber who installed the shower.*

"My house is flooding," Eleanor intoned, to the mop. "I don't know why."

Lele laughed.

Had she actually called the insurance company a second time, had she heard and said these words? When?

The water remediation company sent a team out immediately. Like Kurt, they were already in the area. She had a distinct sense of déjà vu as she opened the door, this stream of people going in and out of the house, gawking at its increasing ruin.

Early on, Lele had been an inpatient at a teaching hospital, and she'd been generous and unembarrassed, welcoming in students and residents whenever she was asked. "At least my cancer's good for something," she'd said. A small crowd in white coats had paraded into Lele's room, sometimes multiple times a day, to poke and prod at her exposed, deteriorating body.

Water remediation was presented as an emergency: The wet beams and joists would rot away, mold would spread through the house, the house would collapse. Twenty thousand dollars. These numbers had ceased to have meaning. Mere days ago, curtains had felt important. Now Eleanor would dance naked through the house, all the lights blazing. The awning, the stuck key, ridiculous. A functioning shower would be a distant dream. The wrapping and siding and missing wall would have to wait for now, they were like a cancer—ha!—while the water remediation was a severed limb, an artery bleeding out.

Three men had come, dressed in matching yellow jumpsuits, the first to have uniforms. Over two days, they pried up the bathroom tile, smashing it in the process, and cut away the drywall of the entryway ceiling. They set fans and heaters and sensors and industrial dehumidifiers on both floors. Snaking tubes met in the middle, within the first-floor ceiling and under the floor of the bathroom. There was one spot where the carved holes aligned and Eleanor could see straight through, from one floor to the next. The collective noise of the machines was extraordinary, like standing inside a jet engine. The uniformed men wore yellow, over-the-head ear-protection muffs.

Matt finally responded on the morning of the second day, as Eleanor stalked back and forth in the living room and the men worked overhead. She watched a shard of slate tile fall through the hole in the ceiling to the entryway below, shattering on the concrete floor. "Heads up," someone called, too late.

Sorry for the slow response! I've been busy with a sale for another client. I'm afraid I don't quite understand your message and how I can best help you. Can we set up a time to talk by phone? How about this afternoon at 2:55?

He has another call at three, she thought. He schedules his life in five-minute increments.

She took Matt's call sitting in her car, driven out of the house by the noise. The rain coating the windshield blurred the landscape into melting, meaningless shapes.

"The builder is gone," Matt said. "Any plumbers, the siding subcontractor, everyone he was affiliated with. Dissolved, disappeared, out of business. You could get a lawyer and chase after names, but the warranties are essentially worthless."

"Kurt seemed to think my insurance—"

"Kurt's great," Matt interrupted. "The best. But it's in his interest for you to think someone else will pay for all the work you sign off on, that you'll get reimbursed eventually. He gets the business, and you're on the hook for it."

Eleanor did not want to think this of Kurt, who had told her everything would be okay, who had promised to fix everything.

The line crackled with Matt's breath. "I thought you understood the situation, Eleanor—why the house was so cheap. Why you could afford it. I sent you everything before you made the offer."

The water remediation team would leave the earsplitting equipment there for ten days, then return to collect it. On the way out, one of the men presented her with the ruined chandelier. It was much smaller than she'd thought when it had been hanging, festooned in light. It made the intricacy more impressive; the now warped and stained blades of wood were incredibly fine. The fixture was only the size of a human head.

• • •

That evening, Eleanor tried joining a session in the car. She put the laptop on the dashboard and turned on the cab light overhead, hoping it wouldn't kill the ancient car battery. It felt colder inside the car than outside, the air chilled and stale. She wore her jacket zipped to the chin and a wool glove on only her left hand, needing her right to operate the touch pad. The Wi-Fi icon on her computer had only the bottom wedge filled in, and no matter how high she turned up the background blurring effect in her video settings, it was obvious that she was in a car. Her odds for retaining this new client felt low.

Initially, the connection seemed fine, the visual quality almost better than usual. In the client's profile, she had listed her preferred name as Ruthie, and according to her birth year, she was seventy-eight. She looked younger on-screen, a notably handsome woman, her thick white hair blown out and styled, a modern pearl necklace across her throat—five baroque pearls, artfully irregular in shape, on a silver cord. "What brings you to therapy?" Eleanor asked.

"Oh, it's a new benefit of my health insurance, at work." Eleanor made a note that Ruthie was still working, not retired. "We get access to this—thing." Ruthie gestured in a circle, presumably encircling her computer. "Seven sessions a year. And I thought, well, why not give it a whirl? I had a little trouble setting everything up. Do I look okay? Can you hear me all right?"

"Actually . . ." Eleanor tapped the increase-volume key on her keyboard, but it was already maxed out. Ruthie had a frail, whispery voice that drifted in and out, though Eleanor could still understand everything she'd said so far. "You're a bit quiet. Are you able to turn up your microphone volume? Or move closer to it?"

"Let me see—I thought I already—"

Eleanor could now see only Ruthie's hairline and eyebrows, and her voice had dropped away even further. "Never mind. It's okay. Go back to the way you were before. I'll turn on the captions." The auto-generated captions had never worked that well, not even when Eleanor had had faster, more reliable internet at the old apartment, but she figured it couldn't hurt. "Is there anything in particular you want to talk about today?"

"Well, I've been thinking about my husband, lately. He passed away. It was a very long time ago." The captions began to pop up along the bottom as she was mid-sentence, white text in a black strip.

[pass away it was a very logo logo]

"I thought I'd made my peace with it. All the ways it wasn't perfect." Ruthie's voice was cutting out more, every other word fading.

[I thought I'd may my piece Bisquick always it wasn't Bisquick]

"It . . . silly . . . upset . . . someone gone . . . years."

[it steamily to beep set summer gone for years]

". . . hurt his back, and he was never really the same after that. He couldn't work anymore. He'd been such a proud, generous man, and now he needed help with everything. And the pain . . . never enough . . . caught him buying . . . street."

[Curtis Black and was never hilly the same after that he could twerk anymore heathen search a proud generation mama and now he needed help wither thing ah ah pain enough ah cover cower burr street]

Ruthie's audio sputtered out completely. Only a few garbled sounds came through, but from the captions and the motions of her mouth and hands, Eleanor could tell she was speaking more rapidly and fluidly now.

[al pastor was a great comfort to me bracken but sin ten my relationship chore merch has also gotten communicate implicated

and I'm not sure I believe believe believe then everything roundabout wife]

"Ruthie," Eleanor said. "I'm sorry, I think we're having some technical difficulties. I can't hear you at all now. Maybe we should stop and restart the call. I can point you to the help page for your audio settings." The hard rain on her car roof filled in the silence. "Or the problem might be on my end."

Ruthie looked worried. She fiddled with her necklace as she spoke. The creamy luster and rough, lumpy surface of the baroque pearls suddenly made them look, to Eleanor, like teeth.

[testes beef four fiscal I already harmony Walkman through letting up chatbot said I did everything right rites is this going]

"I'm going to leave the call. You leave too, and we'll both come back. Can you hear me? Hold on, I'm going to pull up the chat and send you a message." Eleanor scrolled through the menus. She could never remember how to access the chat window when she was already in a call.

[my heaven fishes essence Eleanor it hurts it hurts so much]

Eleanor stopped clicking. "What?"

Ruthie was still talking quickly, gesticulating. She appeared to say several long, brisk sentences, but only two words appeared in the caption.

[it hurts]

"Are you saying you're hurt? Where?"

[everywhere]

Eleanor covered her mouth with her hands, revealing her single glove to the camera. Composing herself, she said, "Ruthie, I don't know if you can hear me, but I can't hear you at all. Just hold on a second—"

[no get them away from me get away from me]

She had the chat window open, but when she typed, nothing appeared in the message field. Her computer made a beep of protest with each keystroke. "Stop talking," she said, desperately. "I can't hear you."

[you're doing this to me I hate you you're the one doing this to me]

"I'm not doing anything. I don't know what to do. I don't understand what you want."

[why did you give them to me it's hopeless why is it taking me so long why is this taking so long Eleanor make it stop make it stop]

"I'm trying!"

[you gave them to me]

"You told me to!"

[you did it]

Eleanor's eyes squeezed shut.

". . . my seven sessions?"

She opened her eyes. "What?"

Ruthie's face lit up. "Oh, I think I can hear you again! I was asking if this will count as one of my seven sessions, if we have to . . ." The audio cut briefly. ". . . my health insurance."

[oh I think I Kinnear again I was hashbrown fountain one of mile severance]

"I don't know. I'll find out for you. I'll make sure it doesn't."

Ruthie resumed her pantomime, but Eleanor could tell without reading the captions that she was being thanked. Ruthie tilted her head, puzzled, just as the sound returned. "Are you in a car?"

• • •

Unlike prompt, acquisitive Kurt, the water remediation company had not billed her, even as their presumably expensive equipment sat unattended in her house, sucking moisture from the air, the din penetrating the cotton balls she'd stuffed in her ears. She had time to let the enormous figure—twenty thousand—haunt her. What would she do? What people did. Lele had opened a retirement account for her, some years ago, though she hadn't contributed to it since Lele first got sick. Lele had cautioned Eleanor against withdrawing that money so severely it brought to mind a curse, a door in a fable that was never to be opened. She would empty it out regardless. She would put what she could on her credit card. She would take out another loan.

Eleanor looked up Aunt Cece on social media, saw that she was traveling overseas, tapped *like* on a picture of her in a crowded riverside market. On impulse, she sent Antoni a message on a platform neither of them used anymore; his last post had been four years ago, and hers had been five. The message felt impotent and safe, delivered nowhere. A note in a bottle, tossed out to sea.

Thinking of you, she wrote.

The house was at least warm again, as hot air was pumped into the space between floors. She sat with Lele in the living room, mother and daughter facing each other on the two armchairs. It was only four o'clock in the afternoon, but the sky was the color of charcoal, the sun tucked behind the mountain range and an opaque layer of dark clouds.

"Tell me what to do," Eleanor said. Her ears plugged with cotton, her own voice sounded weak and higher pitched, reverberating only through her skull.

Lele's posture was unnatural, her arms and neck flung back, knees spread. Her chin pointed to the ceiling, exposing the soft rolls of her throat. In her own voice, as Lele, with patient calm: *Bisquick Kinnear hashbrown logo fishes summer fountain.*

• • •

The house was small, but when she was at one end, it worried her that she couldn't know what was happening at the other. As she brewed a pot of coffee in the kitchen, she thought she heard footsteps overhead. When she took a mug to her bedroom, she thought she heard the front door opening and rushed back to check. As she tried to doze lying on her side, one pillow under her head and another mashed against the ear facing up, phantom sounds rose through the morass of sleep, forcing her eyes open again: tapping on the roof, scratching on a window in another room. A wet, slurping sound, like a stuck boot being pulled out of mud, the moment the suction breaks. Of course, she couldn't hear anything at all—not over the deafening machines, not through her makeshift earplugs. It was only the pulsing and gurgling of her own body, her hair brushing against the cotton balls, the echoing amphitheater of her head.

• • •

That night, or the next, or the next, Eleanor had appointments at eight p.m. and nine p.m., the last slots offered by the scheduler. Eleanor wore headphones that did little to diminish the incessant roar of the machines on her end, but no client had yet inquired or complained about it—she supposed the background audio suppression technology worked best on this kind of flat white noise, leaving her alone in her madhouse, straining to focus on their voices. She never tried the car or captions again.

Wing-Yen was late joining the first call—fifteen minutes into their scheduled fifty—and when her camera finally clicked on, the video feed appeared as vague, grainy blocks of gray and cyan. Eleanor puzzled out what she was looking at. The wet glint of an eye, a black streak of hair. The top half of a sideways human face in a darkened room. Wing-Yen must be lying in bed, a phone or laptop propped up in front of her, lit only by its glow.

"I don't want to talk," Wing-Yen said, at last. Her mouth was out of frame. "I just want you to count this session and sign off on it."

Eleanor nodded. "There are things we can do that don't require you to talk much. We could do some skill building. Awareness, relaxation, visualizations."

"If we have to."

Eleanor had looked more closely at the Parenting Plan and at the statement Wing-Yen wanted her to sign. She was only attesting that Wing-Yen was her patient, and that they had had a minimum of ten sessions. No diagnosis, no clinical judgment, no claims of fitness or state of mind. Eleanor wondered how Wing-Yen and her husband had come to this agreement, why he would consider this meaningful. Wing-Yen was only promised supervised visits, on a schedule to be determined. Eleanor suspected this was just a stalling tactic as he moved, and they would have to start all over again in a new state. She saw Wing-Yen getting on a plane to sit in a McDonald's, across from a toddler who did not know her, under the watchful eye of Calvin's new girlfriend.

Would Teddy sign the papers out of pity, after ten sessions of silence? She could imagine his refusal, imagine him opining at length on the integrity of process, the value of a man's name. As opposed to the genuine treatment and progress of his embezzling CFO.

Eleanor modeled exercises for Wing-Yen. She named the concrete objects around her. "Chair, sweater, box, lamp, window," she said, omitting the bed and nightstands, which would reveal she was in her bedroom, and the wad of towels. She noticed a new crack in the wall, running parallel to the window—not a crack but a thin, swollen passage of fluid under the paint, splitting into finer branches toward the ceiling, an artery into capillaries.

She guided Wing-Yen to relax each part of her body. "Spread your toes," she said, "let them fall to the side. Relax your left calf, let the muscle sink away from your shinbone. Now relax your right calf."

She worked her way up to the face, not knowing if Wing-Yen was listening, if it mattered, speaking in a soft, slow drone. "Let your eyeballs sink into their sockets. Let the corners of your mouth spread away from each other."

Wing-Yen's eyes were closed. The camera was out of focus, the static worse without the whites of her eyes to reflect the screen. A gray lump in a cyan void.

Eleanor's voice thinned to a whisper, vanishing under the machine din, impenetrable to her own headphones. She let the exercises jumble, let her talk run to nonsense. Picture your thoughts as a clicking pen, she said. Release the pen into a river. Your husband is a bird. Let go of the balloon. Name all of the colors you hear.

"You are tied to the bed," Eleanor said, inaudible to herself. "The ropes are only cobwebs. Get up and break through."

• • •

A new client intake session at nine p.m. Instead of preparing, in the ten minutes between calls, Eleanor checked her phone, stared at the walls. More branching veins, engorged with water, snaked down the sides of the light well, just below where the rain thrashed upon the skylight.

As they greeted each other, Eleanor was distracted by her new client's background. Rows of tightly packed desks with computers were visible behind him, some divided by privacy screens. He wasn't wearing headphones. "May I ask where you are?"

"I'm at work," he said. "But nobody else is here right now." Jared had a sparse beard and hair that grew straight out, like a lion's mane, from his narrow face.

"Are you at risk of being interrupted? Generally—"

"Nah, it's fine." His video had the same blue cast as Wing-Yen's, in the cool, sterile light of his office.

"Maybe there's a conference room you could use, with a closed door?"

"I said it's fine."

She noticed the puddle under her bedroom window had spread such that it touched the corner of the duvet hanging off the bed, the water wicking up the white fabric. Her throat felt dry from monologuing at Wing-Yen. "Okay. What brings you to therapy, Jared?"

"I want to practice talking to females."

She swallowed. "Yes, um—there is definitely work we can do related to that anxiety. Could you tell me more about what—"

"No, I want to *practice*. That's why I picked a female therapist."

The machines on the other side of the wall picked up suddenly, loud to louder, a high-pitched squeal on top of the mounting roar of moving air. "That can certainly be part of it. We can rehearse specific situations you're concerned about, and talk about different ways to prepare and build up your—"

"Cool. And you'll give me feedback?"

"Yes, of course. I think it would be helpful to first know a little more about you and your—your goals and—" Eleanor pressed on her headphones, pushing them against her ears, resisting an urge to shout. "And—and—specific . . . difficulties—"

"My goals," he repeated. "I mean, to get them to go out with me. To not look at me like that."

Was the squeal coming from one of the machines, or was the ringing inside her, the death cry from the cilia in her ears? "Look at you like what?"

"You know. That *look* you all have. Like I'm a worm you want to step on, except you don't want to get your shoes dirty."

The noise cycled down again, to something almost ignorable through the headphones, like a hair dryer or a kitchen vent fan attached to her head. "And you only perceive this hostility from women?"

"I'm not *imagining* it. It's real. You're looking at me like that right now."

"And if I tell you that I don't feel any hostility toward you, that my face looks neutral to me, how do you feel?"

"Like you're a liar."

"Do you believe that women are generally liars?"

"Well, yeah. Everyone knows that. Women will tell you that."

"Who are the women who have told you that?"

"You know," he said again, impatient. "Online." A light in a doorway behind him went off, probably a motion detector in a connecting hallway, but the room he was in remained lit so evenly, so flatly, that there were no shadows, no sense of depth, like he was in front of a green screen, a stock image of an office.

"Where online?"

"*You know*." He said this phrase with strange emphasis, not as verbal filler as most people would, but like he was angry with her for pretending not to know, for playing dumb. "Social media. Live stream chats. Comment sections."

"And these are strangers?"

"They're not . . . I mean, they're real people."

"Sure," she said, leaving that alone. "What about the women you know in real life?"

"Like, on the street? At the gym?"

"Well, say, your mother? Your female coworkers? What's your relationship like with them?"

He scoffed. "Look, I know you think your job is to ask me about my mom and make me cry, but *I'm* paying *you*. This is my time. I paid for it. So we're going to do what I want."

Eleanor felt like all the processes in her body stilled, went silent—her heart, her breath—so she could better hear the house around her. Under the dryers and dehumidifiers and whatever else, she heard a gurgling sound, like a babbling brook, water rushing into water.

• • •

She rose from bed, walked out to the landing, down the stairs.

The front of her house had vanished, replaced with a collapsed wall of red brick, the bricks at the top of the rubble staggered like steps. The water remediation equipment was nowhere to be found. A long conference table now took up the entire entryway, surrounded by plush leather chairs. Matt stood solemnly behind the pulled-out chair at the head of the table. Except it wasn't Matt, it was Vance, the mortgage broker—both and neither of them, in the manner of dreams.

She sat down in front of Matt-Vance and started perusing the large stack of papers on the table. She touched her mouth absent-mindedly as she read, stroking a thicket of wiry hair above her lip. She felt she understood the garbled text, the many-sized letters dribbling off the page. They marked the formation of companies within companies within companies, all with mail-service addresses, easy to dissolve as necessary, impossible to hold liable, and only across a long, snarled, convoluted chain were they traceable back to her.

She felt displeased by the yellowed cream leather chairs, the glass top of the conference table, pocked with fingerprints. She hated ugly furniture. The part of her that built furniture was at odds with the part of her that built houses, or rather, funded the building of houses, the buying and selling of houses. Her furniture designs were minimal, deceptively basic, masterful in their simplicity. She loved to spend long afternoons perfecting the plainest-looking joint, crafting something that could last forever. While the houses, on the other hand—

She looked up at the wall of broken brick. Behind it, she could see a two-story row house, the destroyed wall—the collapsed facade of the house—revealing an open cross-section, like a dollhouse. In the second-floor kitchen, two older women and a young boy cowered in the corner, surrounded by rubble and broken brick, having narrowly escaped being crushed. Dust still rose like smoke, staining their skin and clothes a powdery white.

Beside her, not-Matt-Vance said, *Shared foundation. The inspector was one of our guys. Once we started work on the neighboring place—well, they'll have to sell to us now. What choice do they have?*

She nodded. Soon, it would be time to leave this place, to disappear to another part of the country, with new partners and new plans, while lawsuits and investigations dragged on and failed to materialize behind her. She stood from the conference table and walked to the living room. Plain white shoeboxes were stacked on top of one another, forming neat, even towers, higher than the top of her head. Stacked boxes stretched from the entryway to the kitchen, in two rows, parallel with the walls, with an aisle between them for her to walk. The white cardboard had a glossy, appealing shine. Out of curiosity, she knocked over a tower with her elbow. As it fell, it took out the pile beside it, the boxes and their lids scattering across the concrete floor. They were empty inside.

Not-Matt walked behind her. *Small footprint*, he said. *They go up quick. We're talking weeks.*

In the kitchen, she thought, Oh, this is too much. We went too far. She opened the nearest cabinet, and the doors were made of thin plywood, like a child's play kitchen, already tearing around the back of the knob handle. The counters had been painted to look like marble, the veins dark and unnaturally uniform in color, and the gray wood-grain laminate floors were unevenly laid, the wobbly lines dizzying to look at. Not-Matt had disappeared or stayed behind among the shoeboxes. With her in the kitchen were Kristy, Eleanor's client, and the man she recognized as herself—the bushy mustache and narrow eyes, the self-satisfaction. Teddy's embezzling CFO. She felt apprehensive, seeing him. It's another one of me, she thought. He knows the game. Why would he buy?

I'm buying five of the six, he said. *We're close to the parks, and they photograph well. For short-term listings, that's really all that matters.*

Kristy-not-Kristy ran up to her, clutching at her hands. *Oh my god*, she said. *I can't believe it. I can't believe this is my house! I have a house. Me. I seriously never thought this was possible.*

She pulled free from not-Kristy's grasp, disgusted by her, her neediness, her lack of guile. She turned and the kitchen had fallen away. She stood in a desert, an endless expanse of reddish earth, here and there broken up by prickly, defiant, silvery brush. Boots had appeared on her feet, and she could feel the heat of the earth through the soles. The sun seemed to fill the sky, more white than blue, cooking her eyeballs in her skull, crisping her skin.

Matt-Vance had reappeared at her side. *Paradoxically*, he said, *your problems here are water access and monsoon season.*

She loved this landscape, the raw potential of it, owning so much of it for cheap. She was god on the third day of Genesis; she had made the heavens and the earth, light and darkness, called forth the dry land from the seas, but she had yet to add flora and fauna, craft a little Eden for mankind. She loved the killing heat, the feast-or-famine rain, a stark reminder that life boiled down to survival of the fittest, a game of winners and losers, masters and fools. And she was a winner.

Where she stood with not-Matt, the shadows at their feet were shortened and stark under the scorching light, hers still taller and broader than Eleanor's could ever be. She watched not-Matt's shadow morph and twist as he became someone else. Teddy.

Not-Teddy said, *Sometimes I dream their dreams.*

And then, of course, she was looking down upon the valley, the valley as Eleanor had never seen it. Still forested, a steep-sided bowl where mountains met, the rim aglow with pink sunrise, the air sweet and clear. She was hiking up a path formed by a fallen tree, which had skidded lengthwise down the mountain like a sled after being felled by wind or lightning, leaving flattened ground in its wake. A path then tamped down by animals, soft with whispery new growth. A path that quite possibly no other man had ever trodden.

There was no Matt-Vance with her, no one to tell her a good idea from a bad one. The desert hadn't worked out the way she'd wanted—she'd left a ghost town of repeating houses around a half-finished community center, the pool just a pit dug out of the crumbling red dirt—but she'd gotten out in time, still made money in the end. And she loved the valley even more than she'd loved the desert. Lush and verdant, unclaimed. Hidden for all of history from the civilizing hand of man, an opportunity that no one else had recognized, a virgin green jewel, all hers. All his.

Eleanor woke to a short, sharp clang that rose above the racket of the drying machines, the rain, the cotton plugs in her ears. She would later realize the sound marked the end of the rattling in the kitchen—whatever was broken inside the exhaust fan had finally been torn free by the wind, clanking as it landed inside the metal air shaft. Into this muffled soundscape, her mind added the TV show theme from her childhood: *Now you know how the world works. Now you know how the world works!* Like everyone else, she was doomed to dream the dreams of the man who built her house, the men who ruled the world.

17

Eleanor was lying in bed, awake, uncertain of the day or the time or when she'd last slept, when her phone vibrated and lit up by her head. To her surprise, it was Antoni. A message in a bottle returned. The length surprised her more, several lines in the narrow cartoon bubble.

It's so good to hear from you! I've been thinking about you, too. I wanted to reach out so many times to see how you were doing during lockdown, and then when I heard about your mom. But I wasn't sure if you wanted to hear from me, and I didn't want to make things harder. How have you been?

She wondered how he'd heard. Teddy hadn't. And all their friends, back then, had been Antoni's friends.

She felt a violent, dizzying rush of hope. Lele was sitting under the window. Eleanor hadn't changed the towels that day, and they dripped from one corner onto Lele's hair and the shoulders of her quilted jacket. He's probably married with two kids by now, Eleanor thought. He probably moved to the other side of the world. Lele didn't have to say anything.

Eleanor: *It's been tough, honestly.* And then, as its own, second message: *I miss you.*

He replied immediately. *I miss you, too.*

She leapt out of bed. Without knowing why, she pulled the cotton from her ears, and the roaring machinery in the house reached her brain at full volume. She paced the floor at the foot of her bed, phone in hand. The display in the corner indicated it was just before midnight. Finally, she wrote: *Could we get together for coffee and catch up?*

She watched in dismay as his status went in and out of *typing*, as he deleted and restarted his response several times. She'd gone too far, apparently.

That might be tricky

So he was married.

Antoni: *Any chance you could come over for dinner instead? Maybe tomorrow?*

She felt delirious.

I would love to. She remembered suddenly, uneasily, her earlier premonition that his mother had also died, that they had been orphaned together. *Do you still live at the same place? At your mom's?*

Again, he typed and backtracked for a few minutes, but the message she ultimately received was only one word. *Yes.*

• • •

The following day, she canceled her afternoon and evening appointments, something she had never done and dimly acknowledged was unwise when she desperately needed the income and positive ratings. The process required no explanation, only x-ing them out in her scheduling tab. The platform would send form apologies.

Eleanor had not showered in an unknown number of days. Less than ten, she supposed, since the water remediation men had yet to return. Her clients couldn't smell her, or tell that her lank, greasy hair had solidified into the shape of the low bun she wore at the neck.

She had a client with a badly behaved dog, who felt her neighbors and everyone she passed on the street was judging her when she took the dog on walks. She had a client who felt tempted to cheat on his wife and didn't know how or if he should talk to her about it. She had a client with two teenage children, both going through severe psychiatric crises, who wanted someone cheaper than their doctors to talk to for herself. She had many, many clients experiencing a nonspecific, ever-changing malaise, tired and anhedonic and meandering in their speech, for whom she could do nothing but bounce them back to prescribing physicians, apps, worksheets, self-help books, cite the same handful of studies at them, let them tread and retread their memories, searching for something to blame. She had too many clients—she knew this, that she wasn't forming the kind of relationships and concrete therapeutic plans that she had in the old days, the Before days, in that shared office with Teddy. She found it hard to invest in them, when they didn't come back; and perhaps they didn't come back because she didn't seem invested. Her responses were getting increasingly generic, blander and blander, for fear of mixing up the specifics of different lives. She thought this was the fault of the platform, somehow, but also thought that no one else would agree. Any other sensible person would say she was simply bad at her job.

She washed her hair in the sink of the downstairs powder room. She used the plastic vegetable-washing bowl and a washcloth to soap and wipe off her body as best she could, standing shivering and naked on the concrete floor. She had noticed another thin, dark line at the base of the pedestal sink, where the floor was perpetually wet, but she was ignoring it. There was a growing crack in the floor where the living room opened into the kitchen, originating under the built-in bookcase, and she saw no reason to investigate that either. She had washed and dried a load of towels that morning, and a sulfurous odor hung around the washing machine like an omen.

She looked at herself in the mirror above the sink, which cut her off at the top of her rib cage, not unlike the framing of her webcam. She was ghastly thin, her breasts triangular and slight, almost pubescent. Wet and relatively clean, she could see that her hair seemed finer than before, had lost the wiry, exuberant thickness that Lele's had had into her sixties, up until she got sick. "You could sew sutures with our hair," Lele used to say. Eleanor didn't look, she thought, like a woman in her prime, or like an old woman—she looked like a little girl with some horrible, precocious aging disease that ravaged her face and stretched her proportions. Her periods had always been irregular, but she realized now she couldn't recall the last time she'd had one. Sometime in the blurred, contiguous stream of time between when Lele died and when she bought the house. She couldn't remember more precisely than that.

But the hope remained, like a palpable weight in her mouth, a thing she could taste and turn over with her tongue, a peach pit with the last of its flesh. She put on jeans she hadn't worn in years. The rigid denim seemed to hold her upright at the waist. She felt a giddy, long-forgotten nervousness as she tried on sweaters and considered the minute differences in how they draped, how the colors reflected upward onto her cheeks. She settled on a navy cotton crewneck that had fallen out of her video-call rotation for not being warm enough, because of how the fabric felt on her skin—breezy and sensuous at the same time. She set her damp hair into one long braid.

Lele was leaning in the passage to the kitchen when Eleanor walked past, her face again in an unfamiliar configuration, an expression that made her look unlike herself. *Don't go*, she said, the voice thin and tight, strangled of air. *This is a mistake.*

Eleanor tried and failed to ignore her, to stare straight ahead. Lele shook her head slowly, with an air of condescension and resignation—like a parent who has decided to let their kid fall from the jungle gym to teach them a lesson. *I told you not to climb so high*, her face said. *You never listen.* The very opposite of Lele's parenting philosophy in life.

Eleanor had thrown away all her makeup in the move, discovering when she went to pack it that everything was expired, clumped, discolored, shattered inside cases. Her raincoat and boots carried a fungal smell from never drying out completely, but this seemed to her the smell of everything outside everywhere, and couldn't be helped.

• • •

The ruts left in the road by Richie, Jaclyn, Kurt, and the water remediation truck had filled and overflowed. Eleanor's little hatchback powered through the standing water and up the steep hillside, across exposed patches of mud where the gravel had washed away.

She stopped when she came upon a deer, standing in the middle of the mountain road in the rain. In the beam of her daytime headlights, the doe's belly was heavy and distended, making it look almost like some other kind of creature. A camel, a donkey, a kangaroo down on all fours.

She tapped her horn. The deer slowly turned its head in her direction. Eleanor read, in the long taper of its face, the emptiness of its black eyes, a sullen stubbornness, an air of refusal. She honked again, more aggressively, and jerked the car forward a few inches. The deer took three small, mincing steps forward, still partially blocking the road, and resumed staring into the dark, dense woods. Eleanor crept past tightly, almost brushing its tucked tail and backside with her car.

• • •

The house Antoni shared with his mother was in an older neighborhood on the south side of the city. It was a shame, Eleanor thought, driving along the streets of closely packed homes, the asphalt bulging and split from tree roots, that the weather had driven everyone inside. In the summer, the sidewalks were full of families, children riding their bikes and playing until the last light of day.

Antoni and Frannie lived in a former fisherman's cottage, the kitchen extended into the porch and an addition tacked on sometime in the last hundred years. It was neighbored on one side by a stout fourplex and, on the other, by another small cottage with four cars and a boat trailer crammed into the driveway. Frannie's overgrown garden and tall grass looked appealingly wild in the rain, lush and green more than neglected.

Antoni opened the door as Eleanor was still coming up the walk. He stood framed in the doorway, waiting, giving them time to observe each other as she closed the distance, like a bride walking down the aisle. She remembered always thinking he looked tall in that low-ceilinged house, the doors proportioned for earlier, shorter generations. He had the same haircut he'd had when they were together, if slightly shaggier—a squared-off crest now streaked with silver at the front, gone completely gray at the temples. He wore khakis and a plaid flannel open over a T-shirt, an outfit he would have worn in his twenties that did look dated, but endearingly, comfortingly so. He had aged well. He looked fundamentally unchanged.

"Eleanor," he said, in greeting, as though confirming to himself that it was her, and how she loved the sound of her name in his mouth. Teddy and Mira called her "E," Kurt called her "ma'am," and no one else called her anything. "Get in here. Get out of the rain."

So much was as she remembered it, as she stepped inside: the butter-yellow fridge in the corner by the front door, Frannie's love of decorative plates and plastic flowers, the perpetual smell of a hot meal cooked in animal fat. But another smell struck her immediately, one Eleanor associated with people who owned too many pets—ammonia, soiled bedding, chemical deodorizers. A television blared in the adjacent living room, which surprised her, as Frannie had always been vehemently against owning a TV. "We used to have one, when the boys were young," she'd explained, once, "but as soon as their father passed, I got rid of it. Nothing but bad news and trash. I prefer to get my gossip from my girlfriends."

Eleanor felt herself mirroring Antoni's shy, downcast smile. She resisted the urge to embrace him. "Let me hang up your jacket," he said.

"Thanks. Where's your mom? I want to say hi."

He finished placing her jacket on a hanger in the hall closet before responding. "She's in the living room. Let's go together."

The large, sleek flat-screen felt anachronistic and out of scale with the house. The matching love seat and armchairs, upholstered in rose-patterned fabric, were the same as they had always been, crowded together on a small, rose-patterned rug. Frannie had her back to them, seated in one of the chairs. The TV, teetering on a dresser dragged from another room, dominated the tight space, the effect made worse by the commercial that was playing as Eleanor and Antoni walked in—an offscreen voice screaming about the need to invest in gold.

Antoni knelt by Frannie's chair and touched her arm, rather than announcing himself. "Mom," he said, "Eleanor is here. Do you remember Eleanor?"

Frannie glanced over her shoulder. She smiled widely, revealing several newly missing teeth. "Of course I remember! Eleanor, it's so good to see you. Come over here."

Eleanor squeezed into the claustrophobic room. "Hi, Frannie. It's good to see you too."

From her chair, Frannie grabbed and squeezed Eleanor's hand, her grip startlingly strong. "Antoni," she said, staring searchingly into Eleanor's face, not looking at her son, "could you make some tea while Eleanor and I catch up?"

"I—um—is that okay?" His question was directed at Eleanor.

"Sure," she said. She extracted her hand and sat in the other armchair.

Frannie watched Antoni's retreating back. "You know, he wanted to go by 'Tony' when he started middle school. I put a stop to *that*."

Eleanor had heard this story before. "Thank goodness," she said, smiling.

Her gaze returned to Eleanor. "You are pretty as a little doll. I've always liked you, you know. After the first time he brought you home, I said, 'Don't you let that one get away.' Especially after that horrid woman he was with before. Jess. You know about her?"

"I do."

"She was a nightmare. So pushy and rude. Trying to call the shots in *my* house. And *vulgar*. Covered in tattoos, a laugh like a horse. I figured the second they were married, she would throw me into the street and pawn the silver."

"Antoni wouldn't let that happen."

She clicked her tongue. "You never know. That witch had him under her spell. To think that she was the one who called it off, like she could do better than my boy." She patted Eleanor's hand. "But now you're here, so it all worked out for the best in the end."

Antoni returned holding a mug with a tea bag steeping inside. He placed it on the end table at Frannie's elbow. "What is this?" she said, frowning. "We have a guest. Make a pot. And use proper teacups."

"Oh, that's okay—" Eleanor began.

"Are you staying for dinner?"

"Yes, I—"

"No one told me." She put her palms down on the arms of the chair, beginning to push herself up. "I haven't even started cooking."

"Mom, it's okay. I made dinner."

She stared at Antoni incredulously. "*You* made dinner? Why would you make dinner? What's wrong with my cooking? What else do I even have to do around here, besides make dinner?"

Antoni was unfazed. "Dinner's ready," he reiterated. "Would you like to eat at the table with us, or would you like me to make you up a plate to eat in here?"

Unable to find the leverage to stand, Frannie gave up, flinging her weight back into the chair. "Why would I want to eat in *here*, all alone? You and that bitch wife of yours are always doing this to me, Chicco, trying to push me out, take over everything—"

"I'm Antoni, Mom. Not Chicco." Chicco was the nickname of Antoni's older brother.

Frannie's thoughts raced visibly behind her eyes. "I know that. I know who you are! Stop trying to confuse me."

"So you'd like to eat with us?"

Frannie closed her eyes. "No. I can't stand to look at that woman, the one who stole you away and turned you against me. Tell her to leave."

Eleanor stood. "Maybe I should—"

"She doesn't mean you," Antoni said. "I'll bring you a plate in a minute, Mom. Mind the tea—it's hot." He gestured for Eleanor to follow him back to the kitchen.

• • •

After Antoni brought Frannie her dinner, he served himself and Eleanor at the kitchen table. The TV was loud enough to be heard between the connecting rooms, though Eleanor could not make out what Frannie was watching; it seemed like an endless stream of commercials.

Antoni had set out a tea light in a jar, a bottle of wine, and two smudged, dusty glasses. He'd made two of Frannie's recipes—tagliatelle with bacon and olives, and a lemon and arugula salad, both made exquisite by how long Eleanor had gone without real food. "Today's a good day for her, believe it or not," he said.

"How long has she . . . ?"

"We don't know. A year or so since we really noticed. Around the time it became clear she would need full-time care, I was laid off, and even if I hadn't been, we couldn't find anywhere or anyone halfway decent that Chicco and I could afford. Roberta—Chicco's wife—suggested that they just pay me to do it. Two birds with one stone."

Eleanor couldn't think of anything to say that wasn't one of the automatic lines she used with her clients. *That sounds hard. Are you able to take time for yourself? Are there people in your life who can support you? Are you interested in receiving a list of community resources?* "Is Chicco able to visit?"

"His whole family comes a couple times a year, but he has to time it with the kids' school breaks and his and Roberta's vacation days. Whereas I have all the time in the world," he said, grimly.

They were quiet for a long moment.

"Your mom," Antoni began, abruptly, and then stopped. "It was . . . cancer?"

"Yes."

"I'm sorry. But you probably know all about this, then. Caregiving."

Eleanor nodded. She felt uneasy, wanted to steer the conversation somewhere else.

"I feel like we're at the age when everyone in our generation should be going through this," he said. "But I don't know anyone else who is. My friends' parents all seem to be doing fine—even some of their *grandparents* are healthy and independent. And I can tell they find it terrifying to talk about, to so much as see me and acknowledge what my life is like." He stared into his untouched glass, the red nearly black in the faint candlelight. "I saw Jess. I'm sorry—is it weird to bring her up?"

"No, go ahead." *Please, go on.*

"She said maybe it would be better for both of us, for me and for Mom, if I found a new job and hired somebody, if I moved out. We could go back to being mother and son, and not—whatever we are now."

Eleanor could imagine suggesting this to a client, but not to Antoni, and it was advice she never would have taken herself.

"But I can't imagine abandoning her here, to the cheapest stranger I can find. Even if I could make it work financially somehow." Antoni shook his head suddenly, like a wet dog. "I'm sorry. I feel like I've forgotten how to have a conversation. I'm always doing this. I just spill my guts to whoever will listen. How have you been? What's new in your life?"

Eleanor speared a piece of pasta on her fork. "You never used to cook," she said, ignoring his question. "This is as good as Frannie's."

"I cooked sometimes," he protested.

"That's true. You came over and cooked for me a lot in the first few weeks we were dating, to trick me into thinking it would be a regular thing. And then you just leaned on Frannie."

"She kept insisting I bring you home. She adored you. 'I love to watch that girl eat.'"

Softly, Eleanor asked, "She can't cook at all anymore?"

"Not since she set her bathrobe on fire."

There was a moment that could have gone either way, the air between them heavy with sadness and absurdity, and Eleanor felt her eyes sting. But instead they laughed. First Antoni and then Eleanor in quick succession, out of proportion to anything said, laughing until they were out of breath, laughing until they ached.

• • •

Through dinner, they shared the last of what they'd heard about friends they both never saw anymore—they had a kid, they got divorced, she moved to Cleveland, he went to Turkey to get hair plugs, she kept trying to recruit me into an MLM—and told the pandemic stories everyone had—Frannie insisting on using bleach to clean their groceries, wiping down each side of a cereal box; Lele keeping a dresser drawer full of cash; the line at the stadium where they both got their first vaccine shot; Frannie and her friends hollering and cackling in lawn chairs spaced six feet apart in the driveway. They avoided the present, the more recent facts of their lives.

They rejoined Frannie in the living room. Antoni again greeted her with a hand on her arm. The tea was untouched, and the food on her plate had been rearranged and mashed together, such that it was hard to tell how much she'd eaten. "Tell Roberta to leave," Frannie said, her eyes on the screen. "Tell Chicco to come back with just my grandbabies."

"Roberta's not here, Mom. This is Eleanor."

Frannie perked up. "Eleanor! My goodness. What a lovely surprise. And here we have no sweets in the house. I'll never forgive myself for not baking today."

"But you did," Eleanor said. Antoni looked at her with alarm. She sat down on the sofa, her knees almost touching

Frannie's, while Antoni remained standing. "You made a tiramisu."

"I did?"

"Yes, you remembered it was my favorite. We each had a big slice, and then you packed up the rest for me. I said I couldn't possibly take it all, but you said I wasn't allowed to leave without it."

"That's right." Frannie settled back into her chair. "That's right," she repeated. Her eyes softened, contented. "You know, my tiramisu isn't a tiramisu. Whipped cream instead of eggs, and instant coffee. Cream cheese, the greatest sin of all. My mother would think it was a travesty."

"I love it, Frannie."

"I know. You're a good girl." Frannie blinked slowly, her eyelids drooping. "You have to stay for breakfast. I'll make donuts in the morning. Antoni's always trying to run away, goes in and out at all hours without so much as a hello or goodbye. Now that he's all grown up, with his fancy degrees and his fancy job, he has no time for me."

Antoni's face crumpled. He turned away, stacking the tea mug on the plate unnecessarily.

"Antoni's not going anywhere," Eleanor said. "He's right here. We're both here."

"Apple donuts. It must be apple season."

"You're right. It is."

"We used to have an apple tree in the yard. Apples would roll into the road, get under people's tires. Even when they split and rotted, they smelled divine. The store-bought apples just aren't the same. Mealy, a flat sort of sweet. You have to cook with them. They're no good to eat as they are."

"You do wonders with them, Frannie."

"I should make donuts for everyone. The whole neighborhood. Maybe we could have a little party."

"That sounds great."

Her eyes closed completely. "Tell Chicco to bring me my grandbabies," she murmured.

"He will. They'll visit soon."

They watched Frannie until she began snoring softly, undisturbed by the TV screeching in her face about discount air travel. Antoni picked up the plate and gestured for Eleanor to follow him back to the kitchen. Only the hood light over the stove was on, the tea light blown out, the corners of the room in darkness. He added to the pile of dishes by the sink, turned, and kissed Eleanor hard on the mouth. He tasted of lemons and garlic, of the past.

18

Eleanor waited in Antoni's bedroom as he put Frannie to bed. Even sitting on top of the covers, she was lulled by the bed, the warmth of the room, and she fought to stay awake. Alone in an enclosed space, she again worried that she smelled, that her clothes and the folds of her skin had taken on the implacable stink of rain and death. When he finally joined her, she asked if they could shower together, surprised at her own audacity.

At first, the bright, unforgiving light of the bathroom was a horror, their skin mottled pink and white and brown, bare as plucked chickens, duplicated in the long horizontal mirror over the sink. White plastic grip bars had been screwed into the walls. They did not speak. But the shower was small enough to necessitate Antoni folding Eleanor completely into his arms, pressing the length of their bodies together, his fingers skimming across her wet back. She felt the wonder of seeing his face now, at this age, ghosted by a mask of his younger self. She felt a painful longing—a kind of inverted nostalgia—to see what he would look like through the rest of his life, to see his face in old age, to be one of the few people who could connect all his selves together in a line.

Back in his bed, in the dark, they felt like strangers. In this way they had changed; they did this differently now. Fumbling and tentative and curious, unexpected in the means of their delight.

• • •

Eleanor woke and sensed it was morning, though the darkness was broken only by a streetlight through the thin curtains, haloed by falling rain. Antoni was awake beside her. After a moment, she could make out the shine of his eyes.

"Where do you live now?" he asked. "I always pictured you in that same apartment, settling into the couch with Lele every Sunday, but maybe that hasn't been true for a long time."

"I bought a house."

"That's amazing," he said. His excitement sounded genuine. "Congratulations!"

"It was a mistake." It was such a relief to admit this aloud that she started to cry, the tears hot and sudden, as though they'd been lying in wait.

She talked then for what felt like hours, though the night didn't progress outside, the darkness steady, no sliver or glaze of sun or moon. She began by itemizing all the ways her house was falling apart, the hole in the entryway ceiling, the destroyed bathroom, the open wall in the kitchen, the maddening noise of the drying machines, the crack in the floor, the water coming in everywhere; she jumped back to the day she made the as-is, no-contingencies offer, pressured by Matt, exhausted by the long, fruitless search with Mary; she told the story of the land developer, as relayed by the grocery store cashier—*bang!*—and made frantic mention of disconnected images as they occurred to her: Richie holding her hand in his fist, the rat on the space heater, Oakedale wiped from the earth.

Antoni was quiet, caressing her arm as she lay ranting into his chest. When she finally quieted, her voice hoarse and her eyes swollen, he said, "Move in with me."

"What? I can't do that." Eleanor felt wrung out, confused. "Maybe I made it sound worse than it is."

"Your house isn't livable. Your contractor said so. You're going to damage your hearing, if you haven't already. You don't have a shower. You don't have *walls*. Just stay here."

"But you—we—we hadn't seen each other in years before tonight, and—and Frannie . . ."

"My mom loves you. You're one of the few people I'd trust with her." Antoni sat up, gently pulling Eleanor with him. "Why don't you sell the house?"

"It's a wreck. Who would buy it now?"

"One of the people who fought you for it in the first place. So you sell it at a loss, maybe even a big loss—at least you'd be rid of it, before something else happens."

"I'll be in debt. *Deeper* in debt, and now with nowhere to live." I'm dreaming again, Eleanor thought. This conversation isn't real. "All of the money my mom left me will be gone, with nothing to show for it. She worked so hard, her whole life, and as soon as she was gone—"

"You'll have somewhere to live. Here. And so you're in debt. Everyone's in debt. Lele shielded you from real life, and now you're out here in hell with the rest of us. But you'll figure it out. We'll figure it out together."

"Antoni—"

"This would be a huge help for me too. I won't make you take care of my mom. I'll do my best not to interfere with your work. But just to have someone here with her when I run errands—I can't begin to tell you what a difference that would make."

Eleanor had not known that she was so starved for touch until she was reminded, tonight, of what it was like to be able to run your hands over someone freely, to bury your face in their neck when you couldn't bear to look them in the eyes any longer. She didn't want to go back. The thought that she might not have to, that she could leave the house to rot out there in the valley, off-load it directly into Matt's hands, who would probably love to turn it around for another commission—she wanted it so much. Too much, she could tell. The kind of wanting that destroyed you in the end. "I'll think about it," she mumbled. "Let's both think on it. Do we need to get up soon?"

He nudged his phone on the nightstand. "It's only three. We can go back to sleep."

She feared she would start crying again, just from learning that the night wasn't yet over. She dove at Antoni with an open-mouthed kiss, trying to enclose a sob within.

19

When she woke a second time, the darkness was grainier, inflected with watery gray light. Antoni had rolled onto his side, his naked back to her, his breathing deep and even. She wrapped herself around him from behind.

"Stay," he murmured.

"I want to," she said, into his hair. Her sense of unreality persisted. Anything said in this drowsy space didn't count.

"I'm sorry about the way things ended between us. I'm sorry for the things I said. Your relationship with your mom was special." He sounded half asleep, speaking from a dream.

"It's okay. It doesn't matter anymore."

"Were you alone?" he asked.

Yes, she thought, immediately. Always. "When?"

"Taking care of her."

"Her cousin Cece helped at first. She used to be a nurse." She felt something coming unknotted inside her, beginning to unspool. "Mom had surgery first, and then targeted therapy—these giant pills that each cost a fortune, that weren't covered by her insurance. And when none of that worked, she didn't want to do conventional chemo. The cancer was everywhere already, and she didn't see the point. Aunt Cece was there for all of that."

From Antoni's breathing, she wondered if he'd slipped under, gone back to sleep. "Once she started refusing treatment, they prescribed her a whole bunch of drugs for symptom management, including painkillers. Strong ones. My mom's family had a thing about painkillers—her dad and her brother both died addicts. Mom would never take them, not even ibuprofen for a headache, not even when she got her wisdom teeth removed. Not even after her resection surgery, which was hell for all of us. She took the other pills, but she would insist she didn't need the painkillers, and then she would beg us for them. She and Cece fought about it a lot. Cece said they only worked if you got ahead of the pain, if you took it before things got really bad, but Mom always wanted to wait. I felt like—she's dying, let her do it the way she wants to. What does it matter now? And I think Cece was just angry at her for stopping treatment in the first place. She was convinced it was too soon to give up."

Eleanor spoke softly, almost whispering. "Cece started saying Mom didn't *know* what she wanted, that the pain and the tumors were preventing her from thinking clearly, that it called into question all her decisions, and Mom screamed at her in this way I'd never heard her scream at anyone. Not, like, how she yelled when I got in trouble as a kid. This shrill, wild screaming. Mom said that was exactly why she wasn't taking them, that she needed to stay sharp to take care of everything, because people like Cece were trying to take advantage of her. She threw things. Broke things. Cece said this was something that happened with pain. The violence and the paranoia. She said it was a symptom we needed to report to Mom's doctors.

"And then Cece . . . fell. She tripped over the footboard of the bed. Maybe Mom pushed her. I wasn't in the room when it happened, and they wouldn't talk about it. Cece left and never came back. After she was gone, my mom told me she didn't want the painkillers at all anymore. Not to give them to her, no matter what."

Antoni had gone very still.

"It was worse at night, for some reason. That was when she would come to me, gasping and crying and pleading. At first, I would give her the pills, but then, in the morning, she would be furious with me. So I stopped. I just held her. She would hit me, kick me, call me names, say I was killing her. She thought I was the devil, she thought I was her father, she thought I was everyone who had ever been cruel to her in the past. I just held her. She was so weak by then, there wasn't anything she could do."

It had felt so good to tell him about the house, not to be alone with her shame any longer, to lie here with her feet tucked around his calves, her arms around his torso from behind, his body so warm beneath the covers, finally thawing the ice that had settled in her core. Reassured by the texture of his skin, the topography of his body—here smooth, here hairy, here rough.

"One morning," Eleanor went on, "she seemed like her old self, cheerful and clearheaded, and she told me she was ready to die. She didn't want to go on like this. She told me her only hesitation was that she couldn't do it herself, and she didn't want me to get in trouble. I told her I didn't care. I would do whatever she asked.

"All of her prescriptions were only given a few days at a time, a week at most. I was constantly at the pharmacy. I had stopped filling the ones for painkillers, but she made me start again, so we could stockpile them until we had enough."

The hair at the back of Antoni's head was soft against her cheek, his muscles taut under her stroking fingers. Taut, tight, tightening. His chest rising and falling faster, the dream turning, changing shape. "She had me burn the notebook she used to keep track of her meds, of what she took and when, as though someone was going to check."

Her fingers curled into claws, holding him against her, her fingertips pressing hard enough to indent dough. She could no longer pretend he was asleep. "She told me who to call, what to say," she said. "She asked me to wash her hair."

Don't go. This is a mistake.

"She wanted to wear her favorite pajamas."

Antoni rolled over to face her. She knew this expression—it was the one Lele gave her on those terrible nights of withholding, her eyes bulging and white and full of accusation. It was the look you give to the devil.

Frannie's voice rang out in the hall, the shuffling of her slippers as she passed Antoni's closed bedroom door. "Chicco! Chicco, get up! You're going to be late!"

Antoni sat up at the other side of the bed, pulling on his clothes from the day before. He didn't look back at Eleanor until he was fully dressed, his hand on the doorknob. He stood there for a long moment, shadows of a dozen emotions crossing his face, possibilities blooming and withering on the vine. She could feel the person he'd seen, the person she'd been through the previous evening—someone who shared his memories of better days, who made him laugh, someone he wanted to take to bed, someone he trusted with Frannie, someone he welcomed to live in his home, someone he would save from the wreck she had made of her life, someone he could love—vanish, leaving the real Eleanor behind, the sheets pulled to her chin, the reek of wet rot rising from her skin and the pit of her mouth and her blackened heart, a stink she could never wash away. "You should leave," he said, at last.

20

The city receded, the highway unfolded: the distance sign for Bering Rock and Oakedale, the welcome sign, the railway track to nowhere. Vindictive rain fizzed and crackled on the windshield, like the hiss and pop of a wood fire, like frantic applause. Cars threw up blinding sheets of water whenever their tires crossed pits in the asphalt. Traffic lights danced and swung like beads on a string.

I told you not to go.

Eleanor stopped at the same grocery store. The store was again deserted, and the same woman was working alone, but she seemed not to recognize Eleanor, her manner distinctly cold. Eleanor wondered if she had imagined their first encounter, imagined the cashier's voice rising in morbid excitement, her fingers at her throat. *Bang.*

She scanned Eleanor's purchases—instant meals, protein bars, earplugs, toilet paper, eggs—and spoke only to announce the total. "$103.57."

Eleanor took out her wallet and ran her thumb along her credit card, momentarily at a loss. Her lips felt chapped and raw at the edges. From being kissed. She looked up at the cashier. "What's your name?" she said.

The woman tapped the name tag on her apron, bemused.

"Stella," Eleanor read aloud. "How's your day going, Stella?"

"Same as most days around here."

Ask me my name, Eleanor thought. Ask me about my day. "I can't remember a time when it wasn't raining," she said. "I can't remember the color of the sky on a sunny day."

"No such thing," Stella said, wryly. "It's always raining. It's always rained." She gestured with her chin. "Use the PIN pad."

Eleanor pressed on. "It's such a shame about Oakedale. Did you know anybody there?"

"I know *everyone* there." Slower, enunciating sharply: "One. Oh. Three. Fifty. Seven."

• • •

The mud on the private road off the mountain pass was slick, sucking at her tires, drawing her helplessly downhill into the valley. The rust on the swing gate had spread more than halfway across, devouring and scabbing over the neon yellow. The other homesites looked like shallow, discolored pools, like those used for industrial cooling—perfectly level with one another, just brimming over, pockmarked by falling rain.

The rises and falls in the grading of the gravel street were highlighted by where it dipped underwater and where it surfaced, where she could park. As she slowed the car to a stop, her headlights reflected off an opaque whiteness in front of her that trailed and curled at the edges, a wall of low-lying fog. An image was projected onto the fog from an unseen source: two human shapes, a couple. Lele and the land developer, standing posed together as though for a portrait, shoulders overlapping, the shorter Lele slightly in front. The two suicides. Eleanor turned off her lights and the fog disappeared.

Somehow the native ground cover and cedar chips in the front yard absorbed enough water to leave patches of exposed ground. She jumped between them like stones in a river.

She lifted the garbage bag over the front door to unlock it. The wet tape was beginning to loosen and slide. As soon as she opened the door, she was assaulted by the noise. She took a set of earplugs from her groceries, opened the package, and put them in her ears, disappointed to find they were not much better than the cotton balls she'd used before. She could still distantly hear the churn of the machines, and the internal workings of her body were only amplified, but she was deaf to the small, shuffling sounds she made as she removed her coat and shoes. She wouldn't be able to hear someone sneaking up behind her, or hiding in another room, the vibrations in the air that warn of what's ahead.

She brought her groceries to the kitchen.

As soon as she passed the bookshelf, stepping over the crack—longer than yesterday, terminating in new, smaller cracks—she felt as though her brain had shorted out, refusing to process what she was seeing, accept it as real, identify and name each element of the scene before her.

Her kitchen, the cabinets painted different colors with different handles, the open shelves with her mismatched dishes, the removed window leaning on the wall behind the island. The plastic sheeting had torn from where it was nailed in one corner, and the loose corner flapped in the wind, like the entrance to a tent. At the base, a puddle encroached from outside, the water extending inside a few feet, deep enough to appear transparent, to give wavering reflections of the appliances and the light.

A deer buck stood in the center of the room.

She could not hear him, of course, if he was making any sound. Only her thundering heart. His nostrils flared. His right ear twitched, flattening and popping straight up again. But he was otherwise as motionless as the doe she'd seen in the road the day before, only much, much larger—larger than she knew deer in the area to be. Or perhaps a deer in its proper context is diminished, dwarfed by ancient trees and sky, while a deer stuck in a kitchen reveals the full majesty of its size.

His eyes seemed unusually far apart, as though facing outward on opposite sides of his head. His antlers were wider than the span of a man's shoulders, and curved inward like a crown, each tine tall and spiked and a gleaming, polished white, not the yellow ivory or velvety brown she'd seen on springtime deer or shed antlers on the ground.

It's not a deer, she thought, clutching the handles of her paper bags, not knowing if they crinkled, how much sound she was making. It's another ghost. I made him. I willed him into being. He sprang from my mind.

One independent eye slid in her direction, the pupil slitted and horizontal like that of a goat. His jaw hinged open, the thin, liplike ridge of skin undulating, and she assumed he was crying out, braying, that her presence had made him realize he was *inside*, trapped, somewhere he didn't want to be.

She instinctively dropped her groceries, flinging them away from her, and dropped low, covering her head with her arms, watching the buck through the slot between her wrists. Watching as his back legs kicked out, as he ran in frantic circles, smashing on his antlers and hooves the glass of the leaning window and the dishes on the shelves, denting the fridge door with his flank as he failed to turn past it. The sound of each plate and bowl and glass shattering upon the concrete reached her only as a tinkle, a *ping*, the highest notes on a piano. She shrank into a tighter ball, dropping the heels of her hands over her eyes.

When she sensed it was over, she parted her hands. She rose slowly. The buck had found his way out. Through the triangular gap left by the flapping sheet, she could see him bounding away from the house in a straight line, crashing through the standing water. He reached the tree line, the near horizon of her vision, where he slipped between the closely clustered trunks, and the forest seemed to close ranks, envelop him, shield him from view.

• • •

She put on her boots. She righted what was left of the window—the nearly empty frame—and set it back against the wall. She swept up the glass and ceramic shards on the dry side of the room, picked up the large pieces with her hands and placed them in a trash bag. She used the mop to push water out through the hole in the sheeting, over the lip of the plywood board. Bits of glass clung to the mop strands, each razor edge sparkling. The floor remained gritty and wet.

Despite the wide, rounded indent in the door, the fridge and freezer still sealed properly. Her groceries had slid halfway across the floor but remained mostly intact. Several of the eggs were whole, and those that had cracked had done so within the carton. She would pick out the shells and cook them later that day.

From outside, she considered the free corner of the plastic sheeting—could she reattach it herself? Nail it back in? Duct tape probably wouldn't suffice. She texted Kurt.

• • •

The water remediation truck returned in the early afternoon. This time, only one man in a yellow jumpsuit hopped out, his yellow ear protectors around his neck. They spoke at the door, the rain falling in a hard diagonal line. "We're stretched a little thin right now," he shouted.

He checked the sensors in the entryway and the bathroom, and then, like it was nothing, he flicked a glowing red switch, turned a handle, and hit a red button, and the noise—like a miracle—wound down and died. Her breath shuddered as she exhaled. Glorious, luxurious silence rushed in. But so did the cold, an instantaneous change in the air, the cloud of heat the machines had been pumping into the heart of the house seeming to dissipate immediately.

"It's as dry in there as the rest of your house," he said, his voice echoing, rich and sonorous in the new quiet. "Which means I can pull all the equipment. But I recommend you get some consumer-grade dehumidifiers, and of course, solve the root cause of the water intrusion."

For the rest of the day, she checked on him between client calls, as he took everything down on his own. He was short and stocky, a cube of yellow, and four of the machines were quite large, two upstairs and two down—each the size of a clothes dryer or a dishwasher, such that he could barely get his arms around them. He ran past her in the hall with armfuls of cables and tubing, trash bags of tile and drywall. Sweat poured down the sides of his face as he inched sideways down the stairs, leaning back against the railing, pressing one piece of equipment or another to his abdomen. She wondered what she would do if he fell.

At dusk, his jumpsuit darkened in the armpits and collar and down the back, they met again in the entryway, where he passed her a clipboard and a pen. He wheezed when he breathed, and she tasted a sympathetic tang of iron in her throat. "Do you want some water?" she asked. He shook his head.

Twenty-nine thousand dollars.

"The guys on the first day said twenty," she said.

"Yeah," he panted. He coughed wetly into his elbow. "The tile took longer than they expected, and you needed an extra fan. And taxes and fees, you know. But your insurance is paying for it, right?"

"No."

"Really? You should call them and get that sorted out. Oh, just a heads-up, your electric bill for this month is going to be insane, but your insurance should cover that too."

She looked up from where they stood, through the hole in the ceiling, through her upstairs bathroom floor, beyond. On some level, she expected to be able to see the sky. She signed.

"Hey, Kurt."

"Hey, Ruben," Kurt replied, coming through the front door, which had been left ajar. "You just finishing up?"

"Yep." He took the clipboard back from Eleanor. "Your guys are doing the restoration here? The bathroom and the ceiling?"

Kurt glanced at Eleanor. "I believe we're still working that out."

"Well, see you on the next one. Have a good evening, ma'am."

"Drive safe," Kurt said.

It took Kurt less than five minutes to nail the sheeting back in place. He came back around to the front door. The garbage bag covering the lock slid to the ground as she opened it again.

"Should stay in place this time," he said. "What happened to the window?"

"Deer," she said.

He looked at her blankly from under his baseball cap, as though she'd made a joke he didn't follow.

"It fell," she said, tired.

"Ah. That's too bad. You're best off getting a new window, then—a new pane will cost just as much."

She tried to nod, but her head felt heavy, bobbing meaninglessly on her neck. "How much for today?"

His gaze dropped to his wet hands as he wiped them on the front of his jacket. "No charge," he said, after a pause. "I was on my way back from another job."

Eleanor knew her house was not on the way from anywhere to anywhere. "Thank you," she said, dully.

"Just call when you're ready to tackle the siding. Or the bathroom. Or the ceiling." He looked at the exposed door lock, the garbage bag at his feet. "What's going on with this?"

"It fills with rain and the lock sticks."

"Ah. You need a locksmith? I know a guy around here."

"Richie?"

"Yeah. You know Richie already?"

Of course he knew Richie. Of course they were all friends. "Yes," she said.

Kurt still didn't move to leave. He shifted uncomfortably, fidgeting with the work gloves he had clipped to his belt. "Have you thought about evacuating?" he said, at last. "The roads are getting dicey, might wash out. My truck barely made it, and I saw that little car you have out front."

I have nowhere to go, she thought. "I'll wait it out."

His brows knitted.

"The storm," she clarified. "The rain."

Kurt looked her in the eyes, something he never did, his own eyes downturned, still frowning—a hint of frustration, of sadness. He wanted to say something he didn't have the words for, or that wasn't his place to say. "Well," he began. "Well," he said again. He stuck out his hand for a handshake, and when she shook it, it seemed final, conclusive, their business complete, like they both knew he would not be back to do the siding, the bathroom, the ceiling. She watched him hurry through the downpour to his truck, the cab light turning on and off as he jumped inside. She shut the door.

• • •

Kurt gone, she lay down on the living room rug, between the pale wooden chairs and the pale wooden coffee table. That afternoon, she'd had a new client who, unprompted, had told a story of being abused as a child in vivid, gruesome detail—a single night when her father had almost strangled her to death, and then killed their kitten by crushing it under his boot. The client had then hung up, only twenty-five minutes into their first session. Eleanor had messaged her repeatedly: *We seem to have been disconnected! I'm trying to restart the call, but on my end, it appears as though you're rejecting it. Would you like to continue? Are you all right? It's okay if you want to stop for today and reschedule, or if you want to work with someone else. I just want to make sure that you're doing okay!*

Eventually, she clicked the alert button beside the client's name in her call list. Moments later, a pop-up appeared with a thumbs-up emoji: *This user has checked in as safe!* Eleanor had stared at the disembodied cartoon hand for a solid minute. The only button was labeled *Close*. She hated herself for wondering if she'd still get paid.

She had not changed the towels that day, or the day before. The paint around the leaking windows had bubbled, the outer layer sagging like the skin of a popped blister. The baseboards under her bedroom window and the window at the top of the stairs were loosening from the wall, swollen with water, bending outward like the hoops of a barrel. When she stepped in and out of the kitchen, past the bookshelf, she felt a frigid upward draft, as though the crack went through the floor and through the foundation and through the earth, down to some frozen hell.

She'd noticed that the water remediation company—Ruben—had left behind a ladder, in a nearly inaccessible corner of the bathroom. Where the shower had been, around the hole in the floor, the studs and insulation had been left exposed, along with the connection points for the fixtures and the reedy, feeble-looking pipes. Already, she could hardly remember how the room had looked before, a few intact, scattered slate tiles the only reminder. If they noticed the missing ladder, they could come back and get it. She wasn't going to say anything. For $29,000, she could have a ladder.

Down on the floor, she wondered who had bought this rug, and from where. If the developer had picked it, or if he'd hired someone to pick it, or if he'd hired someone who hired someone who picked it. Or if it had come so late in the process, when he was desperate, that it came from his own collection, if it had once softened the floors of a luxurious mansion in some faraway place. She could feel the cold concrete on her back through the short pile. She tried not to think of Dr. Culver's rug. Her thighs ached. She let herself think of Antoni.

She heard Frannie walking along the stairway landing above her, back and forth, calling for Chicco, telling him he would be late for school. Frannie's alive, Eleanor told herself. A kitten small enough to fit in one hand jumped up onto Eleanor's stomach, eyes huge and adoring. She reached to pet it, and found the fur on its back was matted and sticky and wet.

She listened to the rain.

21

Eleanor woke with an acute sense of wrongness. She was on the floor still, on the rug, wedged between the coffee table and the wood-frame armchairs. She pushed herself up to sitting. She was unused to the silence, she thought, having lived ten days in the thick of the noise. Or she was disoriented from sleeping on the floor and not in her bed, her ribs aching. Or she was unaccustomed to the house itself, still expected to wake in her old apartment.

She stood. Her legs wobbled beneath her. Her right hand throbbed, her fingers seemingly stuck in a fist, too tender to uncurl. She must have slept on top of it.

The feeling would not shake. An absence, something stolen from the room. An uncomfortable presence, something newly there that shouldn't be. The clean smell of cut wood struck her, absent the earthy, dank smell of wet sheetrock and moldering towels. An uneven sound rose and fell, akin to someone whistling in another room, through a wall.

She wandered to the entryway, cradling her sore hand to her body. The quality of the gloom, the visible shapes of the furniture in unlit rooms, suggested it was past dawn.

A hole was smashed through the window beside the front door.

She thought immediately of Richie. Richie-Culver the giant, the man at the bar in the baseball cap, the land developer, Teddy's CFO, her client's father stepping on a kitten—no, just Richie, tall Richie, Richie the locksmith. She saw it like a memory: the dented, champagne-colored sedan parked at the top of the hill, his long, loping figure descending the gravel road, his upper lip lifted in a sneer.

He was here with her, somewhere in the house.

She patted her pockets, looking for her phone. She dashed back to the spot where she'd slept, listening for movement, and checked the table and the floor. Her phone wasn't there either.

She crept back toward the front door. She would make a run for it, then. To the car. Peel away, tires screeching. But her keys weren't where she'd left them on the entryway bench. Her boots were by the door, where she usually left them, but the rest of her shoes weren't where Kurt had shoved them against the wall after he'd first cut into the ceiling.

The ceiling.

She looked up.

The ceiling was intact. No gaping hole to the bathroom above, floor joists exposed. The wooden chandelier was as she remembered it from the first day she saw the house, dozens of honey-colored slats carved to sit around the glass bowl. A thing of beauty that she had wanted to own.

At her feet, at the base of the broken window, lay a yellowish, faceted rock, the size of a baseball. One of the rocks that formed a decorative border around a bed of ferns in her front yard.

In their front yards.

She instinctively reached for the rock with her right hand. She winced, inhaling sharply. She picked it up with her left hand, feeling its heft and hard edges. It was almost, but not quite, too heavy for her to lift.

A memory, a true one this time: She remembered wrapping her hand in the sleeve of her sweatshirt. She remembered going to punch the window, expecting her fist to go right through, like in the movies. She'd hesitated at the last second, her body tensing and holding back in anticipation, an involuntary jerk backward as her knuckles hit the glass. The force had radiated painfully up her arm. The pane juddered in place and didn't crack.

She remembered groping along the ground with both hands, one injured and one uninjured, her hands settling upon this rock, slick with rain. Yanking it up from the dirt. She'd reared back and thrown it with her right hand, adrenaline holding the pain at bay, adrenaline making her stronger, angry at her first failure.

She looked down at her arm. A few faint, tiny, already-closed scratches ringed the thickest part of her forearm, from when she'd reached through the jagged hole to turn the dead bolt.

She lowered the rock back to the floor, not letting it drop. She turned and started up the stairs, stumbling and catching herself on the first step. Her legs still felt unsteady, as though she had recently been at sea, or as though the steps were a fraction of an inch taller or shorter or deeper than the day before, some difference invisible to the eye and treacherous to muscle memory.

The towels were gone from the window at the top of the stairs. The baseboard sat flush against the wall, flat and dry, as it had been at that first viewing, when she'd watched the other potential buyers arriving and Matt had whispered urgently in her ear. The window then, of course, had been on the other side of the landing, facing the other way.

She went to the window. She had no idea what she would see.

• • •

She looked out to the mirror house, with its white window frames, the total absence of curtains and blinds, rain sluicing down the unprotected front door. Standing in the corresponding window, she saw herself. Eleanor. In the navy-blue sweater she'd worn to Antoni's, her hair in a neat plait, pale and slight. But somehow more substantial than she had felt for the last year. Less like a ghost. Her cheeks fuller, less bloodless, touched with color. Her back straight, her stance wide and firmly planted.

She watched the other Eleanor step away from the window, disappear into the house. She reappeared through the downstairs windows flanking the front door, as she took the last two stairs with a little jump. There were other people with her in the entryway, Eleanor realized, a pair of figures at the edge of a window frame that she couldn't make out.

The front door opened. Eleanor stepped out first, trailed closely by two others. First Matt, in another tieless, close-fitting suit, shirt unbuttoned at the collar.

And then Antoni.

Eleanor and Matt talked excitedly, while Antoni opened a large umbrella with a handle shaped like a duck head. They proceeded down the front walk, Antoni at the rear. He held the umbrella high above their heads, managing to shield all three of them.

They walked unhurriedly to their two parked cars. Beside Matt's sedan, other-Eleanor and Matt shook hands. Matt made a gesture like he was erasing a chalkboard with his hand, wiping something away. Eleanor couldn't hear them, but she imagined she could read his lips. *Easy*, he was saying. *It'll be easy.* He got into his car alone.

Other-Eleanor and Antoni watched Matt's car pull away, as a light, ordinary drizzle fell around the dry bubble of their shared umbrella. When it was out of sight, at the top of the hill, they turned to each other. Antoni took Eleanor's chin in his hand. Window-Eleanor projected a voice onto the gentle, silent movements of his mouth. *I'm sorry*, Antoni said. *I was just shocked, at first. I understand completely. You honored your mother's final wishes. It's not your fault. None of this is your fault.*

Other-Eleanor craned up, standing on her toes to kiss him. A long kiss, the umbrella dipping slightly to the side, blocking window-Eleanor's view.

The umbrella righted itself, making the couple visible again.

Let's go home, said the Eleanor in Antoni's arms.

• • •

Movement in Eleanor's peripheral vision tore her gaze from the window. The door to the spare bedroom—the room that in her house was a spare bedroom—had fallen slightly ajar, just enough to see inside, a sliver of the room. To see a shadow on the floor, irregular and vaguely round, the shape of a fried egg.

A shadow, or a stain.

She turned back to the window, away from the cracked door. Daylight had receded in the moments she'd looked away. Eleanor and Antoni had gone. More remarkably, the rain had stopped. A clear night unfolded across the valley, velvety black, moonless but denser with stars than any night she'd ever seen, the nebulous contours of the Milky Way slashed across the sky. Without the rain and the shrieking wind, she could hear crickets chirping, the rustling of animals in the woods. Sound carried long distances, uninterrupted. She might have been able to hear the church bell in Bering Rock when it rang. Without the rain, the valley felt like an entirely different place.

She could hear approaching cars when they were still on the mountain road, see their headlights flashing in the few gaps in the solid wall of trees. Music poured at top volume from the open windows of one of the vehicles: a pop-country song with a driving bass line, pounding kick drum, anthemic vocals.

The cars appeared at the entrance to the gravel road. Two pickup trucks and a little beater like Eleanor's, driving in a pack. The truck at the front careened at speed around the tight turn, one rear tire dipping into empty space at the last instant, like an animal losing its footing. Somehow all three cars made it to the bottom unscathed, parking between the two houses in the same formation in which they'd come. The headlight beams and the music died with the engines. The cars had more heads than seats, a chorus of shouting, raucous voices. She couldn't see their faces.

She took a step backward. The door to the second bedroom now hung invitingly open.

Inside, the light switch was where her hand expected it to be. The room had been built as a woodshop: The bench in the center of the room had a stack of planks sandwiched together in a vice and a compact table saw running perpendicular at one end. The walls were lined with cabinets and drawers, a pegboard of hand tools. Woodcuts were arranged standing upright in a bin like an enormous vase of flowers. A bright yellow shop vac floated in the middle of the room, untethered, but sawdust and wood curls covered the floor regardless, stirred by her feet.

A chair sat in the corner by the window, the same kind of chair as the ones in her dining room, except the wood was still raw and unvarnished. The seat was chipped at the edges, gouged out seemingly at random. A similarly unfinished barstool—akin to the ones in her kitchen, but shorter, missing the crossbeams between the legs—stood beside it, with an old stereo perched on top, and a steel lockbox tucked beneath.

She sensed she had not been in this room in a while, and that much of the bigger furniture in the two houses—the beds, the dining tables, the armchairs—wasn't made here but in a better shop she'd once had. Whatever was on the bench was an abandoned project, something she never intended to finish.

Sometimes I dream their dreams.

This valley had finally defeated her, nature itself defeated her. The birds and bugs and deer would come to watch her hang. It was a stupid place to build, for many reasons, but where else was left? And wasn't that how progress worked, weren't we meant to fill and terraform every inhospitable corner of the earth, bomb boulders, shave down mountains, raze forests, flood deserts, destroy anything in our way? What cost could there be? What cost had there ever been?

She felt a sense of inevitability about the men outside. A sick sort of pleasure, of relief, that they had come for her at last. Like this was always going to happen. The repressed but never forgotten knowledge of a gambler: that the house always wins.

She hit *play* on the boom box. It was a tape deck, a relic with a metal body, the metal button depressing with a mechanical click. She left a fingerprint in its thin coating of sawdust. The heads whirred a moment on their own before the music began. Tchaikovsky, she thought. The opening strains of Piano Concerto No. 1 in B-flat Minor, op. 23. The tape worn, not quite worn out. Of course she—he—listened only to classical music, to fit his image of himself as a grand figure, a general, an emperor, better and smarter than the peasant rabble, undone now by cosmic, godlike forces and no fault of his own. The sound was tinny, the orchestra overpowered by the piano's entrance, the notes sharp and aggressive, strings harshly plucked. She turned the volume knob, feeling the metallic ridges, choked with more sawdust. The music swelled until it was as loud as it could go, painful to listen to, the faint horns and violins finding presence in the room under the wild force of the piano, drowning out the banging below, the fists upon her door.

Eleanor had pictured this scene many times. But she had never imagined music. First the rallying pop-country song that had played from the convoy, beginning as a low rumble in the distance, growing louder and truer to pitch as the cars approached, the vocalist talk-singing through the verses and wailing in the chorus, a heartfelt cry. Then the sweeping grandeur of this concerto, its urgent, athletic piano, the deafening volume produced by the ancient metal box, so loud she could feel it in her teeth, in her bones, echoing off the walls, louder than thought or the voices on the lawn. Morphing, now, at its peak, into the squawking, anonymous, cacophonous singers of a local TV station children's show, the opening and closing themes together at once: *Now you know / how does / the world work?*

She bent to open the lockbox. Not a safe, but the kind of box where you might keep cash and change at a bake sale. She took the gun in hand. She slid the rack back until a round landed silently in the wood shavings at her feet. She found the now-familiar spot where her throat met her chin, the flesh soft and slack. She pointed up. The tip of the barrel like the press of two fingers.

Bang.

22

Eleanor lay curled on the concrete floor, head in her arms. Her face was directly in the path of a beam of sunlight coming through the hole she'd smashed in the window. She could see the yellow rock without lifting her head, close beside her like a lover's face.

Sunlight, she thought.

There was a muffled sensation in her head, an eerie, rounded silence. She lifted her hands to her ears, thinking she had in the cotton or the plugs, but there was nothing there to remove.

From where Eleanor lay, her gaze was in line with Lele's feet, past the rock, where Lele sat on the bottom step of the stairs. Under her orange pajamas, Lele was wearing the white, knee-high compression socks she'd died in, the ones that looked like something a little girl would wear with a party dress. The feet were soaked through, her toenails showing through the fabric, faintly blue.

You have to go back to your house, Lele said.

"I don't want to," Eleanor moaned, her voice whiny and petulant, a child at the beginning of a tantrum. She rolled onto her stomach, her shirt riding up, the concrete cold against her abdomen. "I don't *want* to." She reached toward Lele, who didn't move. "Mom. *Ma*."

You're late for work, Lele said. *You have clients.*

Eleanor started to weep, and to laugh, and she dropped her face back into her arms. She screamed, muffled by the wool sleeves of her sweater. She stood up.

She left behind the other house, the house with the black window frames. Outside, the rain had stopped, the overcast sky a bright, blinding silver. But as her eyes adjusted, the sky took on a faintly greenish cast, and she could see dark clouds over the mountains, rain falling heavily in the near distance, sweeping over the trees less than half a mile away, visible to the naked eye. The surface of the flooded homesites and sunken gravel roads was speckled and alive. It was raining everywhere except right where she stood. Her hearing still felt deadened, pressure building in her head.

In the land developer's yard, there was still the occasional patch of dry ground, but downslope, surrounding her house, the water was past her knees. She waded to the door, the legs of her jeans like weights, like grasping hands under the opaque brown water, pulling her down.

She looked back at her car. She remembered parking it on a slight rise, a stretch of higher ground between puddles. The contours of the road had vanished. Her car now appeared to be floating, the water to the top of the wheels.

She had left her front door unlocked, but she struggled to open it, the weight of the water against her. With one hard yank, the door swung outward into the flooded yard, and the water rushed eagerly inside with her, spilling into the house. She pulled the door shut again from the other side. It didn't seem logical, to Eleanor's intuitive sense of physics and the physical world, that the water level would be lower in the house, useless barrier that it was. Yet here, the water only lapped at her ankles. The water was strangely still inside, somehow less alarming for being so surreal. Like it was meant to be there, a man-made feature. The entire house a reflecting pool, tinted by the queer green light through the windows.

Her phone was on the entryway bench, alongside her wallet and keys. She picked it up. It had been unplugged—she didn't know for how long—but still had 20 percent of its battery life left.

Lele sat cross-legged on one of the living room chairs, like an image of the Buddha, a wavering reflection below. The water was still lower than the outlets, but the cord of the living room lamp was submerged. Eleanor had the thought that she should unplug it, unplug everything, but she was afraid to touch it.

Eleanor went to the powder room, splashing softly, where the electrical panel was tucked behind the door. She opened the cover and found that the breakers were labeled in chicken scratch, the handwriting so illegible and layered that it could have been another language, and there seemed to be no main breaker at all—but it didn't matter. She flicked them all off, one by one.

Lele was behind her when she turned from the panel.

Dripping, tracking water, Eleanor headed to the second floor. She gathered her laptop, chargers, and what documents she could find into a backpack. Lele had followed close on her heels. *Where are you going to go?* she said. *You saw the car.*

"The car might still run," Eleanor said aloud. But she knew it wouldn't. The water had been higher than the exhaust pipe, higher than the base of the doors. Her engine would be flooded by now.

You're safer here, Lele said.

"I can go on foot."

The water out there is extremely dangerous. It's full of disease, bacteria, sharp metal. You'll get electrocuted. It might rise suddenly and knock you off your feet, pin you down, drown you.

"I can't stay here."

You can't abandon the house. It's all you have left.

Eleanor turned. They were on the landing between the bedrooms and the ruin where the bathroom had been. She tried to grasp Lele by the shoulders, but Lele stepped back, out of reach. "You told me to buy it."

I didn't tell you to buy this *house. Only someone as stupid as you would do that. You're hopeless. You can't do anything without me.*

"You wouldn't say that," Eleanor cried. "She wouldn't say that!"

Maybe not before, Lele conceded. *But I said a lot of things once you started torturing me. When you tortured me until I wanted to die.*

"That's not what happened!"

Lele's face remained expressionless. She turned her gaze toward the landing window, gesturing with her chin. I don't want to look, Eleanor thought, turning the other way, out over the stairs. I don't want to look through that window again.

Below, she saw that the water had risen on the first floor, equalized with the outside. She heard a sound like a bathtub being filled from a tap, and if she strained, she could tell it was coming from the back of the house, where the kitchen was. She could picture it: the water higher than the plywood boards at the base of where the window had been, the weight tearing the plastic sheeting from the staples and nails, pouring in freely.

It's too late, Lele said.

Boots squelching, Eleanor went reluctantly to the warped, stained wall, the rolled towels on the inset ledge saturated and dripping, oozing in streaks, the paint washed away. She stood in the puddle beneath the window.

She looked at the other house. The blank windows, covered and uncovered, the one by the front door with the splintering hole. The road between them was an unmoving river. The light in the construction office remained, fixed as the North Star. Nothing seemed to have changed.

She lifted her gaze higher, farther, to the hills and mountains beyond.

One of the mountains was moving.

The face of the mountain was collapsing, sloughing off. A brown outer layer rushing downward, moving like water, fallen trees and detritus caught in its current. Moving like water because it *was* water, or mud, liquefied earth. Moving unbelievably fast, conquering the mountain's elevation summit to base as she watched. A wall of water, a vertical sea.

Oakedale.

In her mind, a flood happened so quickly that you couldn't see it until it was upon you, blindsided, sucker-punched. You were caught in it and swept away. Or it happened so slowly and insidiously that there was nothing to see—an imperceptible, creeping rise, as she'd been living for weeks. But there it was, in the distance: a flood like an army, a dense battalion on horseback, charging her way.

"What do I do?" she whispered.

Lele had no reply.

• • •

She dialed 911.

She recognized the voice immediately as not human, one of the speech-to-text systems she heard everywhere: a female voice that sounded firm, vaguely reproachful, almost sarcastic. *The 911 emergency response system is currently overloaded. You have been forwarded to an automated triage system. Please state the nature of your emergency now.*

"Mudslide," she said. If it was a mudslide, if literal tons of earth and soil were headed her way, she didn't stand a chance.

Her house would be torn from its foundations. She would be buried alive. "Flood," she amended.

After a pause, as though considering, the robotic voice replied. *I'm sorry. I didn't catch that. Please state the nature of your emergency now.*

"Flood," she tried again. "Storm. Natural disaster."

Lele was still beside her, almost cheek to cheek, pressing her ear to the other side of the phone.

Another long pause. *I'm sorry. I didn't catch that. Please answer the following questions with either yes*—yet another pause, as though the robot were catching her breath, or speaking carefully to someone thickheaded—*or no.*

Are you over the age of eighteen?

"Yes."

Have you or someone else experienced a life-threatening injury?

"No."

Is there an active crime in progress?

"No."

Do you see or smell smoke or fire?

"No—" Eleanor longed to say more.

Your situation may be better handled by nonemergency services. For a full list of nonemergency numbers in your area, visit us online at—

Eleanor hung up. She stared at her phone. A sound burbled unexpectedly out of her throat, neither a sob nor a gasp, like she was already choking on water.

She had four new notifications, all from the virtual therapy platform. A ten-minute warning before a session with David, then a notification that it was time for the session to begin, then a notification that she had officially missed his appointment. This third one had jammed a paragraph of text into the notification shade, ending with an ellipsis, reminding her how easy it was to reschedule or cancel, and that she would be penalized by the client-matching algorithm in the future. The fourth notification was a ten-minute warning for her next appointment, a new client intake.

She knew it was possible to do sessions on her phone, though she never had. Something about it had seemed even more unprofessional, untrustworthy, her phone propped on a mug or clutched vertically in her hand, her client staring at the underside of her chin while she tried to decipher the expressions on their thumb-sized face.

Through the window, a few of the nearer mountains, veiled in fog and cloud, appeared to also be slipping, strange reflections and blurs she realized were new, trickling waterfalls, sudden rockfalls, water pouring from the lower surrounding hills in a way she'd never seen before. She guessed the alpine lakes at higher elevations had overflowed. She couldn't believe how quickly the landscape was changing. The water in the valley itself was undeniably higher than it had been when she'd reentered the house, what felt like only minutes ago: a moat around the opposite house, the hood of her car submerged.

David stood in the doorway to the spare bedroom. He looked like he belonged there, as though the room were his and he'd just opened the door to her knock, waiting politely to see what she had to say.

"I wish I'd joined the call," Eleanor said. "I could have held my phone to the window. You could have watched as the world ended."

Your *world is ending*, David corrected. *The world ends for someone, many someones, every day.* He held up his own phone, the plastic black and battered. *I'll read about you tonight, or tomorrow, or next week. You'll drift by in my feed, another statistic between sixty-second snuff films. Only one, I'll think. One isn't so bad.*

"At least you could have been with me," she said. "I could have asked you to stay on the line with me, so I don't die alone."

Even if I were on the line, David said, calmly, *you'd still die alone.*

• • •

I have to get higher, Eleanor thought. The roof. I have to get up on the roof.

The hallway was crowded with bodies now, people Eleanor had never met in person, people she had mostly failed, bodies merging into one another and sliding apart, the similarity of their faces, their problems, their pain. They chattered to themselves, to one another, in their digitally compressed voices. Kristy grabbed at Eleanor from the top of the stairs as she paced past. *Your house is beautiful,* she said, earnestly. *I love it.*

She felt Jared's spit hit her cheek as she tried to squeeze around him. *You do what I want,* he hissed.

There was no obvious roof access, no attic or balconies or climbable features on the outside. She remembered the abandoned ladder in the bathroom, but it was only an eight-foot foldable stepladder—what she thought of as a normal ladder, a household ladder. From the ground outside, she wouldn't even be able to reach the top of the first floor.

At the other end of the hall, she glanced into her bedroom. Filthy water streaked down the walls. A dozen people were crowded together on her bed, in impersonal, illogical configurations, like a heap of snakes. Among them, she saw the land developer—most of his head missing, but bloodless, the bedding unstained—Lele, Frannie, Wing-Yen, and a young woman cradling a crushed kitten.

"Get away from them," Eleanor said, addressing Lele and the developer. "They're alive!"

Wing-Yen turned her head, which was toward the foot of the bed, her ear resting on the land developer's shin. She looked at Eleanor sideways, just as she had on their second call. *Are we?* she replied.

The young woman was staring at the ceiling, rubbing the dead cat's ear. *You don't even remember my name.*

The water continued to rise on the first floor, swallowing the stairs one by one.

Lele reached out from the bed, beckoning Eleanor to join them. *Someone will come to rescue you*, she said, her voice gentle now, cajoling. Her arms open. *Just wait here, where it's safe.* Eleanor pictured a boat, a helicopter, the military. Some higher authority. Someone, somewhere, tasked with taking care of her, responsible for her life. Lele gestured at the crowded bed, all the ghosts with their faces turned to Eleanor, her clients and their naked suffering, their wasted hope in her. *Someone else will save all of them*, Lele said.

And Eleanor was so tired, her fear transmuting to exhaustion in an instant, her knees buckling under her weight, her skin stretched and cracking as it pulled her bones to the ground. She wanted to believe Lele, this Lele. It wasn't her job, she didn't have to help anyone, she didn't have to help herself. She could lie down and do nothing and everything would be okay. The valley was flooding, the world was flooding, but someone would fix it. Mother, science, government, gods. Someone will save us. She stumbled forward, unsteady as a fawn, and let herself fall into the crowded bed, into Lele's embrace.

She was rewarded immediately with what she really wanted, what she'd wanted all along. The handmade solid-wood bed in the drowning room became flat-pack particleboard on the dry shores of the past. She was in her childhood bedroom, inside one of her earliest clear memories. She had the flu, the first time she could recall being so sick that Lele had to stay home from work with her. But she remembered it fondly—Lele had gathered every pillow, throw pillow, and blanket in the house, including the comforter off her own bed, and piled them onto Eleanor's, the bedding swirled together like a nest, pillows cushioning her from every side. Eleanor was wearing her favorite nightgown, pink with long sleeves and frilly cuffs, patterned with hearts and cartoon rabbits. The fever brought with it a strange kind of euphoria, her senses vivid and heightened, the bunnies leaping gaily off her dress and nuzzling noses in pairs, the printed hearts throbbing.

Lele walked into the room. She looked impossibly young, her cheeks full and round, her bangs curled away from her face, in workwear jeans and a sunshine-yellow T-shirt. She was, Eleanor realized, about the age that Eleanor was now. She put a bowl of thin congee on the nightstand, the rising steam smelling of ginger and chicken broth.

She climbed into the bed with Eleanor, into the mountain of blankets and pillows. "Can you sit up? Do you want me to feed you?"

Eleanor felt well enough to feed herself, but she didn't want to—she preferred leaning against her mother's side as Lele blew on each spoonful and lifted it to Eleanor's mouth. Eleanor was supposed to give a presentation on koalas to her second-grade class that day, and she rattled off koala facts insistently, each one emerging through the feverish haze with seeming importance. "Male koalas have scent glands on their chest," she said, drooling around a mouthful of porridge.

She wanted to stay here forever, nestled in this tiny bed, swathed in pink flannel and the warmth of her mother. But the memory continued. She was suddenly in a doctor's office, staring at her feet dangling off the high, paper-covered bed, the sparkles on her sneakers dizzying in the fluorescent light. Grown-ups were talking in the same room. She knew it was about her, but it was hard to focus on what they were saying, to care about the words. A searing pain lit up the bones of her face, the dome of her skull, her brain on fire.

"The flu this year is a rough one. What did you give her for the fever?"

"Nothing. I thought . . . I thought I'd see if it came down on its own. And then when it didn't, I thought I'd wait to see what you said."

"In general, you can give her acetaminophen or ibuprofen to bring down the fever, before coming to the doctor. Especially if it's this high for this long, or if she seems like she's uncomfortable."

"But that won't help with the flu."

"It'll help with the pain and the inflammation, which will help her rest properly and recover faster."

I'm going to fall, Eleanor realized. She managed to catch Lele's eye as the floor tilted up toward her and her body slumped sideways. Lele rushed over in time, catching and bracing her upright.

Eleanor remembered then the chalky, cloying taste of the grape-flavored liquid acetaminophen, Lele holding the plastic dosing cup to her lips. Why, she thought, had Lele been so easily convinced when it came to Eleanor, but not herself? Why had she insisted on her own unmitigated suffering, for as long as Eleanor could remember, as long as Eleanor had been alive, needing to experience every injury and illness and ache in its full brightness and horror?

• • •

Eleanor was back, now, in her old apartment, standing in the doorway to the bedroom. But the perspective was wrong, somehow warped—the room and all the furnishings were larger than they had been, the doorway itself stretched in all dimensions, the ceiling too high. She held out her hands in front of her. Her fingers were short and pudgy, her wrists cuffed in pink ruffles. She was still a child, still in her beloved nightgown.

Lele was in the bed. Lele as she had been at the end of her life, her body frail, her hair almost completely white. She was sitting on top of the covers—Eleanor's worn, threadbare duvet, unwashed for several weeks—and surrounded by papers, tapping at the screen of her phone where it lay beside her. She let out a cry when she noticed that a pen in the bed with her was leaking ink, a blue blotch spreading on the white.

Eleanor felt someone brush past where she was blocking the doorway to the living room, nudging her aside as they passed.

"Mom, what are you doing?"

Child-Eleanor looked up at the woman standing in front of her. It was other-Eleanor, the one she'd seen from the window, shaking hands with Matt and kissing Antoni behind his umbrella. She wore Lele's jeans, her yellow T-shirt.

"The car title," Lele said. "And I need to call about this bill. The insurance company rejected—"

"I'll do that," other-Eleanor said.

Lele's gaunt, hollowed face made her eyes look larger, doe-like and alarmed. "You have to call about every single one."

Other-Eleanor strode forward. Child-Eleanor was struck, again, by how differently she walked, her straight-backed air of purpose. She sat at the edge of the bed and put an arm around Lele, her hand hovering slightly, keeping her weight off Lele's thin shoulders. "Then I'll call about every single one." With her free hand, she picked at the bedding, frowning at the gritty texture. She looked straight at child-Eleanor, who was startled to realize that other-Eleanor could see her. "Let me change the sheets first. I'll help you to the couch. It'll just take a second. Are you hungry?"

An alarm went off on Lele's phone. Lele turned it off, her eyes lowered. "It's time for my pills," she said, slowly, bracing for an argument.

"Yes. It's two o'clock. You take four of them. I have the schedule in the kitchen." Other-Eleanor was still staring at the small Eleanor in the doorway, who was looking around for Lele's medication notebook. She couldn't see it anywhere.

"I don't want the—"

"Half," other-Eleanor said, crisply. "I called Dr. Wentschler this morning. She said we can cut them in half. You're not going to punch me again."

"That was an accident. I didn't mean to—"

"It's okay. You were in a lot of pain. You were confused. Half."

Now Lele turned to the doorway, too, to the barefoot little girl cowering there, clutching a fistful of her nightgown. "I can't."

Other-Eleanor didn't ask why. She didn't have to.

"I can't lose myself like they did. I have to take care of her," Lele said. "I have to make sure she'll be okay after I'm gone, that I've taken care of everything. That she won't get in trouble for helping me. I have to get her ready." Lele closed her eyes. "I should have been preparing her all along. Her whole life. That should have been my job."

Other-Eleanor swung her feet up on the bed. She gently maneuvered Lele's body so they were facing each other, one hand on each of Lele's shoulders, Lele's eyelids popping open and her gaze directed away from the door, away from child-Eleanor, directly into other-Eleanor's eyes. "Mom. Look at me. I'm all grown up. *I* will take care of everything. It's my turn to take care of you. You can rest now. You can rest, or we can talk, or just be together. We can do anything you want. You can tell me everything you've never told me. You can tell me stories about your life before me. You don't have to worry about me."

"That's all I do," Lele said. "That's all I've really ever done—worry about you."

It's not fair, child-Eleanor cried, a childish plea in her childish voice, welling with childish tears. The Eleanor in the bed had never known Culver. She was the person Eleanor would be if it had never happened. The person she could be if everything were different, if she weren't drowning in a world built out of sugar and sawdust by con men, with no way to succeed, no way out except Lele, her savior, Lele manning the ship, piloting the helicopter, Lele her rescuer. Who wouldn't have chosen it? Who wouldn't have let Lele take over her life, baby her, smother her? It wasn't fair that she'd gotten sick, it wasn't fair that she'd died, that she'd left Eleanor all alone—

"Half," Lele said, hesitantly, from the bed. "But when it's—when I've had enough—will you . . ."

"Yes. There will be enough. I promise. I will make sure they give us enough." Other-Eleanor squeezed Lele's shoulders before letting go. She shuffled some of the papers on the bed into a pile and moved the stack to her own lap. "But for now, you don't have to deal with any of this. I've got it. I'm going to get your pills, then I'll change the sheets and make you something to eat."

Child-Eleanor could hardly stand to look at the two of them, this scene that never happened. Lele now wore Eleanor's nightgown, the kissing bunnies and painted hearts protecting her visible ribs. Other-Eleanor still wore Lele's T-shirt, the color of butter and honey and summer light. The daughter she could have been. The adult in the room.

23

From the wide, doomed bed that had come with the house, Eleanor looked up at the skylight, through the glass, to the discolored sky above. She sensed the ghosts around her, still filling the room and stalking the adjacent hallway, but they had left her alone in the bed.

Soon—in hours, in minutes—the floodwaters would press her against the ceiling, her face tilted up in the last few inches of air. Soon she would swim through the undersea landscape of her furniture, the crushing darkness with no way up at all.

No one was coming to save her.

The ladder might be just high enough to reach the skylight.

She made her way to the remains of the bathroom, the hole that now looked down into the deepening pool of the first floor. Workers had removed the door from its hinges for access, and it leaned uselessly against the wall. Lele—the Lele that haunted this house, the orange pajamas now soaked through and fraying at the hems—grabbed at Eleanor's clothes, fingers struggling to find purchase. *You don't know what you're doing*, she rasped. *You're just going to hurt yourself.*

Eleanor pulled away. She pressed her back to the wall and started to shimmy slowly around the hole. She reached the folded ladder in the corner. It was surprisingly heavy. She had the idea from somewhere that aluminum ladders were light, that other people carried them effortlessly, and she again cursed her physical weakness, the smallness and softness of her body. The smallness was no excuse—Lele, she knew, who was smaller still, would have had no trouble—

But that didn't matter anymore. Eleanor held the ladder with both arms, leaning it against her body as she shimmied back out again, along the remaining strip of subfloor. She felt strangely focused, sure-footed, though her thundering heart betrayed another feeling beneath. So much had ceased to matter in this moment. Her injured hand had gone numb. She heard—or imagined—a sound outside like the roar of the tide, like the ocean had washed a hundred miles inland. Higher, she told herself. Get higher. That's all. Don't look.

She pushed her way through the crowd, the ghosts refusing to part, pushing back, pushing in to be closer to her. She opened the folded ladder beneath the skylight, in a shaft of dilute yellow-green light, as though filtered through sickly leaves.

Remembering her difficulty breaking the window across the street, she dug briskly in the still-unpacked boxes until she found a tool kit that Lele had bought her a decade earlier, in a plastic snap case, that had mostly been used in the intervening years by Lele herself. She withdrew a hammer. She put her backpack back on.

Her feet hit the first rung. Lele tugged again at her pant leg. The fabric was dried stiff at the thighs, still heavy and wet below the knees. *It's too dangerous out there*, Lele said. *Stay here and wait until help comes. Until they come looking for you.*

“Until who comes looking for me? What help?” Eleanor said.

More hands grasped at her as she climbed, guilt, grief, the knowledge she was going to destroy another piece of this miserable, accursed house—the only thing, as Lele had said, that she had left in this world.

At the top of the ladder, she looked down for just a moment. The room was full of ghosts, packed to the corners, but Lele and the land developer were closest to her, holding on to the ladder, faces upturned and shining.

Eleanor strained to swing the hammer straight upward. The angle was awkward, gravity working against her, her bad hand locked in a fist around the handle. Nothing happened. The glass seemed to bend slightly, flexing, bouncing the hammer back at her.

She looked down again. She felt higher than she was, the room distorted, a nervous sweat breaking out along her hairline. The land developer’s ruined face and exposed jawbone were indistinct, ever-changing; he was one man, he was a thousand. Lele wore another expression she never had in life, a wide, flat, open-mouthed, victorious grin, one that bared her gums and her back teeth, each tooth appearing very large and long and yellow.

The water had crested the stairs, a thin wash running into the bedroom.

Eleanor swung again, harder, summoning everything she had. A perfect circle appeared on the glass, cracks like dense spokes in a wheel. The circle was only about the size of a baseball. Tiny pebbles of safety glass fell into her hair, caught in her eyebrows.

She hit it again in the same spot. Larger pieces of glass fell away, rectangular shards that smashed on the floorboards below. One scratched her cheek as it fell, a swift bright streak of pain, as though from a whip.

She pushed aside a few more broken pieces with the hammer, confused as to why she couldn't yet see the sky, and realized there was a second layer of glass. This layer was stronger. She beat upon it with the hammer, making no visible progress, the glass only shuddering in its frame with each hit. An animal desperation rose in Eleanor. She swung again and again. She would not be trapped. She would not die here. The water continued its chase, filling the room, shortening the ladder, devouring the rungs, pulling at her, calling her in the ghosts' many voices. *Stupid child. Gullible fool. The world is too much for you, and you're all alone, of no use to anyone. All you'll ever see is her face as you made her suffer, unable to think for yourself for even a moment. You killed her. You're nothing without her. Now you know! Now you know!*

Finally breached, the upper layer exploded all at once, crumbled to sparkling blue snow, the sound and rush of falling glass startling her almost off the ladder. But she held on, covering her head and closing her eyes. The hammer slipped from her grip and fell. She didn't hear it hit the floor—it landed in water deep enough to sink in, to submerge it with a hushed *gulp*.

When everything was still again, a light rain fell into the room, along with a changed light, the low whistle of the wind.

She looked down. The ghosts retreated to the walls, slinking backward without walking, without using their legs, their eyes fixed to Eleanor. She brushed some of the glass off her clothes and backpack and face, out of her hair, her blood garish on her hands, not yet clotting or oxidizing, red as a candy apple.

She used her bare, bloodied hands to clear away the last bits of glass clinging to the frame. She ascended to the plastic cap at the top of the ladder, labeled NOT A STEP, and scrambled through the hole to the roof.

24

Eleanor landed on her hands and knees in water—of course— pooling on the top layer of gravel on the flat roof. She pushed herself to a crouch, below the low lip that formed a border around the edge. The wind felt treacherous and strong, full of grit.

She looked out at the changed valley. The mountains had stilled, faces reshaped. The treetops at the lowest edge of the forest and the second floor of the opposite house poked out above a murky lake, white scum swirling on the brown surface. A felled tree jutted from the water at an impossible angle. Her car had washed to the embankment below the mountain road, tilted up against the hillside, the right side submerged. The valley, a basin of concrete and gravel, had filled like a swimming pool.

The rain seemed lighter than it had in weeks, pinprick droplets suspended in the charged air. The pressure in Eleanor's head increased, and for a moment, she couldn't hear the wind, cocooned in an unsettling quiet. She remembered, suddenly, the bizarre, pleasant smell of her last visit to the old apartment. She could smell it now, alongside the stronger smells of dislodged soil and wet stone and sewage and plants decayed to sludge, the smell of a flood.

Breaking the silence, bridging it back to the rushing wind, someone was calling her name. *Eleanor.*

She looked over her shoulder. Lele was standing on the roof with her, about ten feet away. She wasn't wearing the floral pajamas she'd died in—she was dressed as she would have for a late fall day like today, in a lightweight down coat, the jeans of her youth, sturdy boots. Her hair was curlier, cropped shorter than she'd ever worn it. She looked both older and younger than Eleanor remembered—older than she'd been when she died, but vital in some unfamiliar way, untroubled as the living can never be.

Overcome, by instinct, Eleanor rose and ran toward her. She was knocked sideways by a gust of wind. Her boots slipped and skidded on the wet surface. She caught herself before she fell. She glanced down over the edge of the roof, seeing the drop to the floodwaters below, whatever hid beneath.

When she lifted her head, Lele wasn't looking at her but into the distance, smiling—another smile that wasn't hers in life, that wasn't anyone's, too beatific, too much at peace. She wasn't the mother that Eleanor had known for most of her life, who had let Eleanor regress into uselessness, who had loved her too much, for whom Eleanor longed even now. She wasn't the cruel, tormenting secret of who she had been at the end, how Eleanor had failed her, how they had failed each other. She was the memory of both, the truth entire. She was only a memory.

Eleanor's palms were imprinted from the gravel, stained and tacky with her own blood. She watched as a last, lingering shard of glass fell from the edge of the skylight frame, tinkling as it broke free and disappeared back into the house.

Lele would have been proud.

Eleanor looked in the direction that the ghost was facing, out over the roof edge, the side of the valley where the mountain road ran along the rim. The slope seemed shallowest, foreshortened by the water, about where her car had washed up. If she could get there, if she swam or pulled herself along somehow, she might be able to scramble up the embankment and reach the road. She could walk back to town. She heard the other Lele, in her mind, reminding her the water was full of dangers, a hundred ways to die. The road might be impassable anyway. It might be no better in Bering Rock. It might be no better anywhere.

The Lele on the roof seemed to see something that Eleanor couldn't, her expression serene, as though the drowned, poisoned development land were some idyllic sylvan landscape—only a lake in the woods. A lake that had always been there, that would be there for the foreseeable future, for an era of geologic time, someday housing rushes and fish and birds and creatures not yet known.

Together, Lele standing and Eleanor kneeling, they watched the rain pricking the surface of the new world.

The ghost held out her hand. Eleanor stared at her dead mother's outstretched fingers. She could still give up. She could drag herself forward on her hands and knees and grasp that hand, as she had on that last, horrible night, into that last, horrible morning, and be led away, back into the dream of Lele's care, into death, into memory, into perpetual childhood, waiting for a savior who would never come. Or she could lower herself down the side of the house—before the roof collapsed, the walls caved in, the flood consumed it whole—into the murderous water, fight her way to the makeshift shore, climb up the sheer face of the mountain road. She'd make it, or she wouldn't. The road would be solid, or the road would be destroyed. She could walk back to town, where her life would be in ruins, homeless and in debt and alone and everything she owned lost to disaster, or until she couldn't walk anymore. Without Lele. As she had smashed through the skylight, as she had surfaced into the open air as the water rose, as she had saved herself. She could go on.

Acknowledgments

Thank you:

To Masie Cochran, an imaginative genius who understands my writing better than I do, and to Jennifer Lambert, who asked the hard questions and believed in this book when there was nothing to believe in. The novel simply wouldn't exist with you both.

To my indomitable agent of fifteen years, Jackie Kaiser.

To Beth Steidle for the perfect cover. To copyeditor Anne Horowitz, who straightened out my bizarre relationship with time and italics, and to proofreader Allison Dubinsky. To Becky Kraemer, Nanci McCloskey, and the extraordinary dream team at Tin House. To the wonderful folks at HarperCollins Canada, Westwood Creative Artists, and Untitled Entertainment.

To Lucy Tan, Danya Kukafka, Susie Yang, Katrina Carrasco, Sonora Jha, Danielle Mohlman, Putsata Reang, Nidhi Pugalia, and the wider literary community of Seattle.

To my family.

To JP, always.

Kim Fu is the author of two novels; a collection of poetry; and most recently, the story collection *Lesser Known Monsters of the 21st Century*, winner of the Washington State Book Award, the Pacific Northwest Book Award, and the Danuta Gleed Literary Award, as well as a finalist for the Giller Prize, the Ignyte Awards, and the Shirley Jackson Awards. Fu lives in Seattle, Washington.